ALSO BY PETER HANDKE

The Second Sword and *My Day in the Other Land*
Quiet Places: Collected Essays
The Fruit Thief
The Moravian Night
Don Juan
Crossing the Sierra de Gredos
On a Dark Night I Left My Silent House
My Year in the No-Man's-Bay
Once Again for Thucydides
The Jukebox and Other Essays on Storytelling
Kaspar and Other Plays
Absence
The Afternoon of a Writer
Repetition
Across
Slow Homecoming
The Weight of the World
The Left-Handed Woman
A Moment of True Feeling
The Ride Across Lake Constance and Other Plays
A Sorrow Beyond Dreams
Short Letter, Long Farewell
The Goalie's Anxiety at the Penalty Kick

THE BALLAD OF
THE LAST GUEST

THE BALLAD OF
THE LAST GUEST

A NOVEL

PETER HANDKE

Translated from the German by Krishna Winston

FARRAR, STRAUS AND GIROUX   NEW YORK

Farrar, Straus and Giroux
120 Broadway, New York 10271

EU Representative: Macmillan Publishers Ireland Ltd, 1st Floor,
The Liffey Trust Centre, 117–126 Sheriff Street Upper, Dublin 1,
DO1 YC43

Copyright © Suhrkamp Verlag AG, Berlin, 2023
Translation copyright © 2025 by Krishna Winston
All rights reserved
Printed in the United States of America
Originally published in German in 2023 by Suhrkamp Verlag, Germany,
as *Die Ballade des letzten Gastes*
English translation published in the United States by Farrar, Straus and
Giroux
First American edition, 2025

Library of Congress Cataloging-in-Publication Data
Names: Handke, Peter, author | Winston, Krishna, translator
Title: The ballad of the last guest : a novel / Peter Handke ; translated
   from the German by Krishna Winston.
Other titles: Ballade des letzten Gastes. English
Description: First American edition. | New York : Farrar, Straus and
   Giroux, 2025.
Identifiers: LCCN 2025028743 | ISBN 9780374616151 hardcover
Subjects: LCGFT: Novels | Fiction
Classification: LCC PT2668.A5 B3513 2025 | DDC 833/.914—dc23/
   eng/20250626
LC record available at https://lccn.loc.gov/2025028743

The publisher of this book does not authorize the use or reproduction
of any part of this book in any manner for the purpose of training
artificial intelligence technologies or systems. The publisher of this
book expressly reserves this book from the Text and Data Mining
exception in accordance with Article 4(3) of the European Union Digital
Single Market Directive 2019/790.

Our books may be purchased in bulk for specialty retail/wholesale,
literacy, corporate/premium, educational, and subscription box use.
Please contact MacmillanSpecialMarkets@macmillan.com.

www.fsgbooks.com
Follow us on social media at @fsgbooks

10 9 8 7 6 5 4 3 2 1

This is a work of fiction. Names, characters, places, organizations, and
incidents either are products of the author's imagination or are used
fictitiously. Any resemblance to actual events, places, organizations, or
persons, living or dead, is entirely coincidental.

πῆ κεν υ πεκπροφύγοιμι

How on earth am I to escape out from under all this?
—*THE ODYSSEY*, BOOK 20, LINE 43

She wanted to start [playing] . . . and progress to a feeling of deep, swollen sorrow.
—CARSON McCULLERS, "WUNDERKIND"

Contents

1. ON THE DEATH OF A STRANGER *3*

2. ON THE LAST GUEST: A BALLAD *43*

3. THE BALLAD OF THE LAST GUEST *149*

THE BALLAD OF
THE LAST GUEST

ON THE DEATH OF A STRANGER

It must have been a quiet day in late summer or early fall. The person in question was on the way to his childhood home. Setting out a couple of days earlier, he'd taken first one plane, then another, and finally, to reach the land of his birth, a third. For the final stretch, as he'd done as a child to get to school, the man had boarded a bus, though by train he'd have reached the agglomeration, a large, densely built-up area, much sooner.

He was looking forward—and how!—to the days ahead, his week of vacation with his parents and much younger sister. And even more—no, in a different way—to the locale, the locality, the village and the woods, the neighboring villages and the new-growth forests—no, not to all that, but to what was left after several decades of rapid development, left in the town centers and on the outskirts, bits and pieces, various "shards," no longer visible at first but nonetheless present, and, he was sure, waiting to be tracked down. But for what purpose? No purpose.

From time to time, the bus seemed to be traversing an expanse of open country far from civilization, on a wide road with hardly any curves. As far as the horizons in all directions, sometimes near, sometimes distant, nothing but nature, with not a human in sight; and he realized he was on one of the old cross-country buses on whose flanks was depicted not the trademarked flying greyhound but an antelope, speeding very differently through the air, if not a dolphin.

So—coming home to evening card games with his father, which usually took place in silence, except for the bids? As it should be. And home to being interrogated by his mother, wordlessly, with only her eyes, the interrogations then predictably giving way to animated storytelling, in the kitchen or on the bench in the courtyard, still there in spite of all the new houses, cheek by jowl, that had crowded in on and eventually squeezed out the farmstead—a wall barely an arm's length from the bench partitioning his family from the neighbors, total strangers but for their voices making their presence felt? His mother's repertoire of tales? Good for her! And home to his sister's accounts of involvements with a succession of men and the pain they caused her, accounts with which she would regale her older brother, her confidant through the years, in the toolshed converted into a one-room apartment: sisterly songs of love and sorrow, this time rendered more intense if possible, or so he'd heard, by the interjections coming from a little fellow just learning to stand unsteadily on his own two feet (ah, the shrinking feeling from the beginning, often verging on guilt, at the sight of all the young'uns, still without any recognizable language, being carried and wheeled along streets and across squares, and especially at the sight of all those extra-large eyes)? Why not? Why not face everything head-on, and even, as mentioned, look forward to it, at least now, while he was still alone on the cross-country bus—actually not old by any means but practically brand-new—and reassured by the sonorous roar of the motor, coming as if from far off, an indistinct roar, at some moments also a clanging, from the depths, from deep underground, and he the only passenger sitting way in the back, in the last row, while the others, of whom there weren't many, were spread out, their heads visible from the rear, here and there? Yes, why not? We shall see. *We?* Yes, we.

He'd had no woman in his life for a long time, and he also had no children, had been living and working for ages—his own—on another continent, or, as he called it, "part of the world." (Let every reader imagine on, or in, which part that would be.) And on that other continent, for this week at home, he'd broken off, from one day to the next, the activity for which, and also from which, he'd been living—that, too, for ages—an activity to which he referred in his mind as "my one-man expeditions." The current expedition had been interrupted just after he'd reached its next-to-last stage and was in the midst of preparations for the last stage. Preparations? Mobilization.

It had seemed to him, while he was still far off beyond the seas, who knows why, that this mobilization would call for a detour once he reached his old stomping grounds. Yet he hadn't pictured what this detour would entail, had at most momentary inklings, without a single image, however fleeting. Nor did he want any such thing. No images, for heaven's sake, and above all no distinct ones! And if now and then he caught a whiff of something "image-like" threatening to come flying to him, behind his back, so to speak, he swerved aside, at least inwardly, as if on a dance floor or in an arena, and the image-arrow zoomed past him. And now, way back in the cross-country bus: he had not even an inkling of what might await him on his so-called native turf, let alone what he'd intended to track down or seek out with which to conclude his expedition. There's nothing more for me at home, nothing at all! he whispered to himself. *And that's exactly what fires you up.* Yes, strange but true. *Or maybe not.* Whatever: I'm looking forward. *Don't spoil it for yourself, playing your own spoilsport, as you often do. Don't trip yourself up, friend; take it one step at a time!* As a passenger, sitting here? *Yes, sitting there, a passenger.*

The bus had long since turned off the highway into the agglomeration. Without warning it kept turning, turn after turn. Yet it seemed as if after every third turn the street was heading out into the countryside again, toward the distant horizons, or, on the contrary, approaching something resembling the center, or one of the centers. Nothing of the sort, however: instead, each time, it ended up on a periphery, never the same one, but also not an off-putting or even hostile one, but rather, perhaps also because of the quite gentle turns, an (almost) friendly one, at least at first glance, an (almost) welcoming one. And it was striking that each of the many high-rise buildings stood all by itself, as did the next one, a lance-throw away, in the "middle ground" by reference to the one in the foreground—in accord (almost) with the rhythm of all the high-rises in the agglomeration—high-rises that at first sight stood "out in the open," to paraphrase the expression used by a poet to describe a far less tall building from a previous century. It made sense that in this New Town, which spread across the landscape rather than completely filling it, the horizontal lines that crossed one another and headed off in different directions, at least those in the background, seemed to be welcoming him, the stranger, or the one who'd become a stranger here, in the form of mobile tangents—local trains, streetcars, even Metro cars as they traversed their aboveground stretches on elevated tracks, all speeding along inaudibly yet uninterruptedly, to connect the most distant housing clusters to civilization. Looking more closely, he recognized here and there the tower of one of the not many but also not few village churches, their towers now at the feet of high-rises and so much smaller than he remembered them from before, as if they'd shrunk. And that, too, was as it should be: that these church towers scattered across the land were no longer so prominent and imperious, pointing toward heaven, if not invoking heaven as a threat. The way they stand there today, hardly noticeable, almost like toys, they seem more, and better, suited to the place. *Toys?* Yes, for a serious game. *Good New Town: You mean?* Something like that.

The bus station, so long and wide that it took up the entire block, in no way suggested a center either, forming instead yet another in the series of peripheries. Waiting in the aisle to get off, as the very last passenger, he noticed that one of the boots worn by the woman in front of him had come unlaced. The woman seemed to be in a hurry, as if any minute now, when the bus's door opened, she would break into a run. He imagined her tripping on the lace and falling on her back, and he approached her, tapped her arm, and pointed out the danger. Was it really a danger? At any rate, she took him seriously and thanked him, both in words and with a look, as if he, the stranger, had just saved her from something terrible that would have been impossible to make right. In that moment he realized that only now, when he'd reached his destination, did he have a face before him, for the first time in his days-long journey. What kind of face? A face. The experience of a face! And the woman, bending over to tie the lace (he was tempted to help, but how?), laughed up at him, the laugh conveying first surprise, then amusement, as she pointed at the man's shoe: a loose lace there, too, though one considerably shorter than hers, posing no danger of tripping, but who knows? What does a stranger like this know? Or what, in this situation and others, did such a woman know? And in his imagination, he saw the woman, since she was already bent over, tying his lace, too, after her own. That didn't happen. But either way, both of them had something to laugh about. That wasn't nothing, and once off the bus and facing the bus bay, empty once the bus had pulled out, he felt he'd arrived in the place of his birth in an entirely new way.

At the same time, he felt his usual reluctance to head straight home. Should he go in the opposite direction, in opposite directions? No, stay near the bus station, sit down somewhere, preferably out in the open, on a bench or the protruding base of a building, with nothing in mind but to perch there for a while. With the passage of time, to be sure: enough emptiness, out-of-the-way-ness, retreating into corners. Back to the hustle and bustle. Which he put into action. Seeing and being seen! And, oddly, less seeing than being seen! Yes, he longed, even yearned, to be seen, and more than merely seen: to be recognized. Recognized by this person and that from the former villages, by a former classmate with whom he'd played football or interacted in some other way? By them, yes, and also by one of the few individuals he'd met later on, during his brief annual visits home, acquaintanceships that because of the time constraints had become friendships more meaningful than all those of earlier years. Being seen and recognized was what he wished for now, on the occasion of this particular arrival, especially by strangers, no, by just one person. *Recognized as who or what?* Recognized. *Also recognized in a bad sense: "I'm on to you"?* That, too.

But no one recognized him—in either way. Not a glance that brushed him, let alone a passerby who stopped suddenly or stared at him wide-eyed: "Is that really you?" And then: "Yes, it is you, it really is!" On the other hand, he didn't see a single familiar face in the crowd, either one from more recent times or one he'd known forever, so to speak, who'd turned up in his dreams, if once in a blue moon. Instead, certain features—a forehead, a nose, lips, a gaze, a hairline—reminded him of people he'd known decades ago, people who seemed familiar, who recapitulated, almost to a T, features of those who'd lived around here. Their descendants? Sons and daughters? And an amazing number of children going by, the spitting images of long-ago playmates: the villagers' grandchildren?

Who did seem to recognize him, at least at first, was a dog, roaming free and probably a stray. Upon catching sight of him, the dog stopped in his tracks and then came toward him, weaving past pedestrians' legs, and, without jumping up on him, trotted along beside him, looking up at him the whole time, until he stopped averting his eyes after every couple of steps and kept them fixed on the dog's, whereupon the dog, large to begin with, suddenly larger than life, did jump up on the man, though without biting, instead letting out a howl, almost a cry, of a sort not to be expected from canine lungs—and suddenly the animal was gone—fleeing? disappointed? disgusted? recognizing that he'd mistaken the man for someone else?

Before the traveler finally headed home, he wanted to check the message on the screen of his pocket telephone. He'd received an alert while on the bus but hadn't looked at it because he wasn't expecting any news, and also, toward the end of his long journey, he was leery of any "notification" or "update."

The message read as follows: His brother, the youngest of the three siblings, was dead. After years in a division of the Foreign Legion that was currently fighting in the tropics, he'd been struck in the head by an "enemy bullet." Killed instantly. "Your brother didn't suffer." He'd been buried that same day—because of the tropical heat. An additional factor was that Foreign Legionnaires, unlike regular soldiers who fell in battle, had no right to have their bodies escorted back to their homeland in coffins draped with their national flag. Attached to the brief message was a snapshot of the freshly dug grave. Prepared with care, veritably staged, the mound with the cross—carved out of palm branches?—and his brother's name, spelled perfectly, inked onto the wood, like the name of a star in the credits of a CinemaScope movie. Huge exotic flowers—*What kind?* Never mind, picture them for yourself—were heaped on the mound (which looked as if it consisted only of the mass of blossoms, the earth underneath hastily smoothed out), and that was the only patch of color in the photo, but what color! Otherwise, far and wide, the land was flat all the way to a dim horizon, nothing but dull gray, against which only the grave stood out; not a bush, not a tree, not another grave in sight, and also no trace of a settlement, not so much as a bird's silhouette. Without those gloriously color-rich flowers, it would have looked as though his brother's grave wasn't somewhere near the equator but in the Far North, in a tundra landscape, sufficiently thawed in the brief Arctic summer for digging a grave, but about to freeze solid again.

For a moment, he saw his brother as a small child, in the one-wheeled wheelbarrow that served in those days as a baby carriage, or more likely as a vehicle in a game that involved circling the courtyard of their parents' farm, with him, the big brother, as the barrow pusher, visible in his memory only from behind. Yes, and then the moment when the little cart, going faster and faster each time it rounded the courtyard, got away from him (known later for his one-man expeditions), gets away from him, and the pusher-less barrow, having reached the edge of the courtyard where it drops off sharply, now lurches down a fairly steep and almost bottomless embankment with the baby aboard and tips into a belt of stinging nettles, almost a forest but fortunately so dense that the fall didn't prove fatal. No trace now of the little brother, vanished into the nettle thicket, and also not a sound. Who can it have been who finally, lying prone, hauled the child, unhurt except for a few burn-blisters on his hands, his face untouched, up into the daylight? He pictured both parents off working in the fields. His sister? Impossible: she wasn't old enough yet to go to school. Or could she have been the one? A neighbor, summoned by my cries for help? Did I even cry for help? And if so, wouldn't that have been the first and up to now last time in my life? Was it a random passerby, a stranger, who immediately pinned the accident on me, standing there silent? Yes, that's how it was, Brother: a stranger rescued you, rescued both of us. But what I'm not imagining but rather am completely sure of, Brother: it wasn't me; I wasn't the one who came to your aid that day, no and again no, in neither word nor deed. A pillar of nettle salt, that was me!

After reading the death notification he'd come to a complete stop, but hardly a moment later set out again for home, taking the route familiar from long ago, resuming his previous pace and rhythm, as though something both inside and outside of him deluded him into thinking that if he kept going, at least for a short stretch, he could undo what had happened, reduce it to a bad joke. He reinforced the original rhythm, making it into a kind of march, stomping along as if he were part of a column or company, taking large strides. But what joined in, or chimed in, as marching songs, seemingly to punish him, were various sayings, repeated silently and all the more viciously, such as: "Today's the most beautiful day of my life!" and "Man and woman, woman and man, together touch heaven, hand in hand!" and "*In dulci jubilo*, I sing with joy and cro-o-ow!" And meanwhile, in front of, next to, behind, and at the feet and head of the marcher, there was nothing but quivering—not merely quivering of leaves and grasses but also quivering of whole trees, whole clouds and expanses of cloud in the sky, quivering of more and more spiderwebs—but why was one of them utterly motionless? Time to set, quivering sun, get out of my sight! But the sun simply refused to set, as if up there in excelsis it were being held back on purpose, not for the benefit of the marcher down below, so he could triumph in a battle of nations or god knows what other world event, but rather, against, and in spite of, him, in order for—*in order for what?*

At some point he noticed that he was lost. In the course of his life, he'd gotten lost time and again, starting in childhood. At first he hadn't realized what was happening; usually, it was others who'd pointed out that he'd gone astray, which seldom upset him, let alone caused him anxiety or fear: he was so confident that a family member or a person responsible for him in some way was nearby, and as soon as he approached that person he'd be on course for home, even if the path didn't lead directly there, meaning to the house. He preferred taking one detour after another with his escort and getting home as late as possible, either arriving when it was almost dark, or not going inside at all, even when the house was lit up invitingly.

Later, after years of annoyance, his own and others', at his "poor sense of direction," when a sense of direction had manifested itself after all, more reliable than that of almost anyone around him, the man wished he could lose his way again from time to time, and anew. He even made that happen, losing his way on purpose, paradoxical though that may sound, as part of a plan. The blind alleys he sought out, which had him sometimes crawling on his stomach, on all fours, or, as in child's play, rolling down a scary slope, grounded and structured his one-man undertakings, and subsequently, enhanced with photos and drawings, determined the form his chronicle of each misadventure took. Being a chronicler of the adventures of one gone astray, whose voluntary and systematic lostness was again not paradoxical, being that kind of chronicler, sharing these experiences, yes, but purely as a chronicler: that was what he viewed as his calling. Narrating, shaping, reshaping, transforming: all that was out of the question for him. "Nothing but authoring chronicles, my own. But for heaven's sake, that shouldn't imply any claim to superior insight!"

Yet it had happened, especially during his expeditions of the last few years, that the chaos into which his insistence on going astray had not so much led as pushed and shoved him, had at the same time become inseparable from him, accompanied by "anxiety and terror, fear and trembling," at least in the latest or next-to-latest episode.

But on the day in question, the man found himself lost there—*Where was that? What did "there" mean?*—on his way home. That had never happened before, not even the first time he got drunk as a teenager, a ghastly experience, which, in his few moments of lucidity, was incomprehensible to him at the time. (Strange, by the bye, the way people who were drunk out of their minds usually found their way straight home somehow or other.)

He wasn't drunk this time, though at the bus station he'd yearned for a glass—no, a whole bottle. Now, however, thrown off his march rhythm, he staggered along like a drunk, someone falling-down drunk. Never would he find his way to the house, the house where he'd been born, the house where he'd lived and worked till he went overseas: never again. To the end of his days, which might come as soon as the following night, he'd be forced to stumble through the strangest of all strange lands, weaving back and forth. But hasn't the route to your home from the station remained much the same over the last half century, just as you experienced it the last time you made your annual trip home, even though almost every inch of the former region of many villages has been built up?

This admonition did nothing to dispel his confusion. Wasn't there an expression, "hopelessly lost"? "That's how it is: I'm hopelessly lost. Just as, in the past, I've remained inwardly perfectly calm, the very essence of calm, in the midst of external chaos such as a hurricane, now, with the outer world seemingly perfectly quiet, shrouded in nocturnal peace, almost dead, inside me everything is in utter chaos." And see the lost man flailing and floundering on the spot, taking a half step forward, another step back, a quarter step to the right, another to the left, and so on?

No, friend, this can't go on. To tell the truth, if you, the lost one, had left footprints on the ground, in mud, let's say—but there wasn't any—or in snow—but how could that be, in summer?—those marks would've resembled a wagon wheel, though a hopelessly broken one—again, hopeless?—or an entirely different kind of spoke-work, such as the rose window in the façade of a medieval cathedral, a rose window in fragments, apparently impossible to reconstruct, shattered by grapeshot or a bomb. With the passage of time, however, in your flailing and floundering, you developed something like consistency—miraculously? Yes, by some miracle. And the prints of my shoes in the mud or the snow yielded the image of a wagon wheel, repaired, and . . . ?

That's how it was, more or less, almost. And instead of "developed something like consistency," maybe say "found a rhythm," one diametrically opposite to the previous one, the march rhythm, opposite in every respect, a good rhythm, not catchy, one that suited the situation: a rhythm that, instead of footprints left behind, suggested a trail leading onward.

And at that a clear vision of the way home came to him, showing every landmark, turnoff, and alley along the route, and stayed with him all the way to the house. At the same time, the idea, or something similar, occurred to him that in his next chronicle he'd report on the rhythm discovered thanks to "going astray" (or the like). *How so: aren't you ashamed of using the news of your beloved younger brother's death as the trigger (or whatever) for that insight (or whatever it was), not to say exploiting it for your projects?* No, he wasn't ashamed, not in the slightest, but was actually delighted by his idea, was proud of it. The only question was how to put it into practice, and, most important, make it concrete, factual, in the language of a chronicle, his language, the language of a chronicler who could leap over the borders of all countries and their manners of speaking.

Before taking the first step, he realized that he'd been standing on one leg for a while, maybe since the moment when the confusion reached its peak and freed him to continue on his way. He executed that first step as a dance step; though it didn't look like one, he felt it as such. At that same moment, the sun finally set, as if on command, as if hastily. And in that connection a line from an old pop song came to him: "When the sun goes down behind the roofs, I'm left alone with my longing . . ." His mother and sister had belted the song out for him in a duet, over and over, to annoy him, make fun of him, because he hated that line, especially the word "longing," which the two singers always screeched two octaves higher.

Taking the shortest route to the house. Night had already fallen, without any transition—"as in the tropics," he thought involuntarily. (Pointless to try to forbid himself such thoughts.) The former farm was reached by one of the alleys maintained by the town, alleys that had once been village, field, or cow-pasture paths, and now had municipal streetlights, if not big-city lighting. Upon reaching his destination, he saw that on the front wall of the house, rather than above the front door, and contrasting with the streetlights, the old courtyard light still glowed, though now without its courtyard, in his eyes a relic of a bygone time: a naked bulb protruding from a white-painted tin plate that served as its neck ruff, splattered—or did he only imagine that?—as always with bird droppings. And another light source—in addition to the house, whose every window was festively lit—directly over the house, against the otherwise pitch-black sky—as black as in the old days—strange!—the first star. For him, as was appropriate for early fall—right?—it represented the Dog Star, the star of ripening pears and apples. And a person like this claimed to be nothing but a chronicler?

Standing in front of the house, or already at the front door, under the archway, on the sandstone doorstep with its fossils of prehistoric ammonites, he hesitated again. Was that a child bawling far inside the house, the sound rendered faint by the thick walls, or was he hearing it in his memory as he stood outside the door? And now the willow-branch broom on the wall, illuminated, seemingly on purpose, by the courtyard light. With just such a broom, his brother had swept the courtyard before dawn to signal his return from his apprenticeship, as he did again when he came back later, by then a journeyman builder—after each absence lasting for days or nights, or, as his father described them, his bouts of gallivanting in the area and beyond its borders. This sweeping outside the house was the first, and remained the only, sound he made after his periodic disappearances, which, in his mother's eyes, and not hers alone, over the years came closer and closer to his vanishing for good. And in idle speculation—again something that came over him against his will—the older brother now saw himself sweeping the alley, as a sign of his arrival. Begone, frivolous fantasies! Get serious, and stay serious!

But how to remain serious at the sight of the welcoming garland above the arched doorway that only now caught his eye, after he'd taken a step toward the broom and then a step back? The garland consisted of a semicircle of spruce branches interwoven with wildflowers, immediately recognizable as the handiwork of his sister, so high-spirited when she happened not to be in mourning over someone or something. (Or thus: even while showing her special brand of high spirits, she had tears in the corners of her eyes, her tearfulness mingled with barely contained rage.) And the height of her high spirits on display here: in an allusion to one of the numerous family legends, crisscrossing the garland's spruce branches and wildflowers were fans of nettle leaves on stems as thick as fingers and as long as an adult was tall, covered from the roots to the pale-yellow umbels with stinging hairs.

The time had come to go in. All he had to do was press the old latch—not a knob, such as the houses next door had, and certainly not a lock with a keypad for a code, if not two or three. Or was the door at least chained on the inside, like a proper city door? No, it wasn't locked; it was just like doors in the old days, if only in the hundreds of villages.

How was the long-awaited visitor greeted? Let only this be mentioned: a shriek, a single one, but what a shriek. It came from his sister, holding the chubby baby, who, startled awake, joined in just as loudly. As a youth, her brother had covered his ears when his sister, barely able to walk, let out shrieks that he felt certain could be heard in the neighboring villages, one shriek after another. But on the evening of his arrival, that one shriek did him good.

Of the meal served to celebrate his arrival and consumed in almost complete silence, let only a few familiar dishes be mentioned, in addition to the wine: extra-large variations on "dumplings" and international "ravioli"; buckwheat flatbreads (in early summer, the buckwheat had been in bloom in that area; was it blue or purple?); and the chunk of butter, still beaded with watery droplets of whey from the churning.

No one spoke except the baby, whose bed stood in a corner of the room where they were having supper. He chattered loudly, in complete sentences, with multiple clauses, the problem being that the individual words were shouted in an unknown, unintelligible language.

Then the child dozed off. Would the mother and sister begin to sing now, softly, softly, creating the right mood for an evening when the family was gathered? Or would the father open the drawer in the table and deal the cards or, putting on his amateur-magician act, reveal them from beneath his hand, if not shake them out of his sleeve? For a long while, nothing could be heard but intermittent gusts of night wind, penetrating the house's thick walls. But then—finally!—the mother and sister—but, never fear, no singing, no duet—began to speak, taking turns: You, Son—You, Brother—have been chosen to be the godfather when this little addition to the family is baptized. The baptism will take place during your week at home. The day hasn't been picked yet—any one of them is a possibility. The child won't be baptized in the new church but in the old one, opened these days only for special occasions. The priest, who stepped down long ago, has a key, and stands or sits in his room, ready from morning to night to celebrate the sacrament of baptism.

From him no response, but the two women saw that none was needed. It went without saying: he would take the baby in his arms and carry him to the baptismal font. And maybe they also picked up, in the barely noticeable bowing of the son's and brother's head, a sign of assent? Or did that result from exhaustion, which now, as midnight approached, suddenly overcame him after all the transcontinental flights and, even more, all the airports?

The truth was that the three others, the mother, the sister, and the father as well, had been waiting all evening, and continued to wait, more and more urgently—yes, waiting could be urgent—for him to give them news and a report on the younger son and brother. With the announcement of the baptism, they had all had in mind, and were eagerly expecting, his announcement of a few bits of information, however meager, from the life of the absent family member. Announcement? Yes, announcement.

In fact, the only thing those still at home knew about the youngest child was this: "He, our Hans, is in the Foreign Legion." They had no idea where, or in what conditions. He hadn't wanted them to hear about him, in any way or under any circumstances. Out of shame? Or for whatever reason. No explanations, all right? The only one, at least from this part of the world, with whom he now and then shared something was Gregor, almost two decades older, and what he shared was insignificant, except for one time, when, in his usual shy way—in earlier times the word would have been "chaste"—he hinted that he'd found "love."

But what they were panting for, including the father, who acted as though he didn't care, was the older brother's account of those meaningless details, or at least one—please! In today's parlance, they were "panting" for news, especially the sister.

On the other hand, it was an unspoken rule in the family, going back generations, that no questions were to be asked. "No questions in this house!" This rule, which had once applied to the whole property—the courtyard, fields, pastures, and distant orchard, bordering on other people's farms—now applied only to the house, or what was left of it. And the new arrival could see all evening long that his sister was waiting for him to open his mouth and give them all a hint, thanks to which the rest of the family could at least have a glimmering of what their "Benjamin" was up to, and how.

In truth, even after he'd been gone so long, the household counted on and dreamed of the return of its prodigal son. It was not by chance that the broom still leaned against the wall by the front door. The older brother—or, as his sister addressed him, without his name, in her letters, her "Dear old Brother"—was welcome, but as an ordinary visitor who could be counted on to turn up once a year. The others didn't miss him. He didn't cross their minds, or if he did, they thought of him as someone who, though thousands of miles away, was always nearby. Even his mother didn't worry about him. No matter what he was involved in at that unimaginable distance, off on one of his "expeditions"—even more unimaginable, if possible—his mother always assumed he was safe. "Nothing can happen to him." Maybe she'd dreamed about him now and then while he was growing up. ("That was all so long ago that it doesn't seem real anymore.") But these days no one in the household dreamed about him and his adventures, and even he sometimes thought of them as "dreamed up."

But they all dreamed about the other member of the household, the quasi-vanished one. "Oh, he's the one who's gone missing, vanished alive." "All the more alive for having dropped out of sight." As if someone who disappeared, went missing without a trace, sparked particular dreams in those left behind, very different from dreams of the dead; every one of those dreams portrayed him living an exceptional life, never against a background of death. The father, almost an old man now, also dreamed this way, not during his dreamless nights but rather during the day, when he sat alone playing solitaire: the immortality of the vanished son?

"Even if pronounced dead, you won't have died as far as I'm concerned." And look, everywhere in the house, from room to room, from bedroom to bedroom, on the walls, on the dressers, on the tables, also in the corner once occupied by the house altar?—no, not there—photos of the absent one. *But not as a reminder of one deceased?* What are you thinking? No, the pictures are meant to conjure him up: "Come back, Son, with you gone, it's as if there's no house; you're the house, you alone!" And that's how it was: not a single likeness of the older brother, no sign of his existence, here or elsewhere, not the slightest keepsake, however trivial, not so much as something put aside or simply left behind from his everlasting childhood. But the other's possessions, especially those from the end of his apprenticeship, item after item, object after object, tool after tool: from the entryway downstairs to the upper floor and into the attic, they were waiting for him: "Come back! You're the master this house is waiting for. The wait's gone on long enough."

Now, as the visitor sat silently at the table, more and more unconvincingly making a show of his (actual) exhaustion, as his parents and sister stared at him, he had to do something to keep them from suspecting the truth. So he tried to think what bit of news, supposedly received recently from his brother, he could make up to calm their fears. But no: making something up—out of the question! Besides, he had no talent for inventing things, or rejected that kind of "flimflam" for himself. What now? He reported, truthfully, merely altering the chronology, that he'd heard "a little while ago" that "our Hans" had experienced "love" "for the first time in his life." What a flash ran around the table, including from the old man, brief and barely recognizable, a momentary flash from the depths of his eye sockets, almost mischievous. No tears, for god's sake! Hold them back at all costs.

The chronicler, in this case a false one (false for the right reasons), now recalled how hours earlier—wasn't it actually days earlier?—upon receiving the news of his brother's death, he'd continued on his way, street after street, at the same time stopping repeatedly to look at the shop windows and take in the goods on display, as if nothing had changed; and how, a little later, as he stood waiting at a red light, with his duffel bag on his back, he'd caught himself covering his face with his hands; they had moved into that position without his knowing it. For a long time, through several red-green cycles, he'd stood there, standing up straight, head in hands. At one point he heard a passerby asking, "Do you need help?" Then a car stopped very close to him and a door was opened halfway, invitingly, and he heard a woman's voice—it sounded like that of the woman on the bus with the loose boot lace—offering him a ride. Both times he'd merely shaken his head.

Now, at midnight in his parents' house, and again contrary to his nature, or what he took for his nature, he saw an image of himself as he'd stood there, his arms raised and his hands motionless, concealing his face like a piece of cloth, a piece of light-colored fabric: an image reminiscent of a scene in an old painting—where would he have run across it?—with a figure standing bolt upright, its face concealed by an actual cloth, falling in folds from the head to the chest.

That old painting was meant to portray someone in mourning—mourning whom, he couldn't recall. And as he sat there in the house and realized that he was about to cover his face involuntarily with his hands again, no, had already raised his hands to the level of his eyes, he promptly dropped them to the table and drummed on the surface. A sign that he had nothing more to report for that day, to be continued tomorrow. The baby in the corner started at the sound. Then silence again, there as here.

His bedroom, with its window overlooking the backyard, was unchanged, as in all the preceding years. The only time he'd come home to find his bed in a slightly different position, or so it had seemed to him, he'd maneuvered it back and forth, here and there, slowly, over the course of hours, till he imagined he finally had it where it belonged and could stand back and admire his accomplishment. Only one item from before was missing from the room: the little wall mirror. It hadn't been taken down and hung in one of the other bedrooms, but had fallen one day, who knows why, and broken. Every time the occupant returned home and entered the room, as he passed the spot on the wall where the mirror had hung, leaving no trace, he would turn his head in that direction and see it reflected on the bare wall. And so it was on this evening. A brief laugh in a moment of senseless, if not nonsensical, trust in the world, such as he experienced in certain situations, the laughter directed at himself against a background or backdrop of something that transcended him personally, a sense of astonishment.

Tired though he really was, he couldn't sleep. Instead, a line from another old hit came to mind, or was it from a poem? A brief sentence in the form of an exclamation, repeated, as the new arrival lay there in the dark, in an endless loop: "How weary and abandoned I am!" He didn't actually feel abandoned at all, but the astonishment stayed with him, a post-midnight astonishment at himself now, at the way he was, or the way he was made, and the fact that he had the gall to be that way, incorrigible.

It had taken a long time for him and his much younger brother to become close. During the younger one's childhood, apprenticeship, and even into his adulthood, the older brother, who from the beginning showed a "morbid" concern for members of the family (that was the term used by his father, who played with more than cards), had had nothing but concern about Hans, and only from a distance, when the younger brother was out of the older one's sight. In Gregor's presence, nothing, nothing at all could happen to his protégé. (*Protégé? Nothing happen? What about the story with the stinging nettles . . . ?*)

Later, when the distance between them had grown so immeasurable that the morbid concern seemed to have subsided, although his younger brother didn't become a stranger to him, Gregor no longer thought of him as his close, even closest, relative but as a distant one, replaced in the meantime by "elective" relatives.

Brotherly love—yes, it did become and thereafter remained "love"—arose and then took shape, a shape with clear contours, unalterable and inextinguishable, during the years when "Hans Benjamin"—step by step, and finally on the verge of steplessness—drifted toward a point of no return, and, by the way, not as the first in the history of the family and the clan. But I mustn't conceal the fact that I, unlike my mother and especially my sister, after a while had almost or completely given up on my brother and didn't waste the whisper of a thought on that loafer and ne'er-do-well, who was causing our parents nothing but shame and, worse still, pain. And my "Him? That's it! Good riddance!" attitude came, more forcefully than from the reports sent to me overseas, from my observations, usually as the only eyewitness, of my brother's absolutely last, ahem, encounters with our mother on either side of the threshold, during my annual week at home. But at this juncture, I'm not going to squeeze any specific details through the portal to memory, as narrow as it is high, not going to inflict any curses on the global interior space known as "memory." Is memory really meant for the roar of war and the clamor of hell? *If not, then for what, please?* For something else.

Now, suddenly, in a flash, brotherly love was there— the real thing. On the evening after his return to the continent beyond the seas—"Damn you, you're not my brother anymore!" (seriously? not entirely!)—he was sitting on the porch of his house, or hut, in a rocking chair, gazing at the Southern Cross or some other constellation. And all at once, believe it or not, out of the clear night sky, a fist hit me on the head, so hard that it felt as though it had bashed in my skull—"I'm dying." In truth, however, the giant blow had come from above and below simultaneously, from outside and inside, and in the next moment, clearly set apart from the previous mindless relaxing, an entirely different kind of calm, the calm of certainty, or, more, of legitimacy, imparted as if by the blow of a sword—the sword not a weapon but the instrument enforcing a law, a law devoid of images, made up entirely of words, issuing a commandment: "You must call up your brother now, on the spot, and invite him to get on the next plane here, so he can accompany you, or you him, on the expedition you're about to embark on!"

And that was what had happened. On the foreign continent, Hans seemed in his element from the beginning. Unlike his brother, who, after decades there, had finally come to feel more or less at home but still saw himself as a stranger at times, and/or also played that role as the one most appropriate for him, Hans showed not a trace of a foreigner's typical uneasiness. Though he didn't speak a word of the local languages, wherever the brothers found themselves on their two-man expedition, he was immediately "in the thick of things," an expression often used in the country from which they came.

Gradually, something else showed up, however, becoming more and more noticeable toward the end of his stay: something like homesickness—which had befallen the older brother only once in his life, at a time now immemorial, when he was still a child, an ache he'd shaken off that very evening. It had been so enormous that another such incident became simply inconceivable. (Did it really?)

But, having had this one experience, he recognized what "homesickness" was—the term had slightly different connotations in every language—and how it affected people around him. *How did he recognize it?* Something else to picture for yourself. Or here's an indication, almost trivial: on their expedition, taking place during the younger brother's first time in another country, from one way station to the next, among the dishes served to him, he began to miss more and more those he was used to from home. Or this: the things missing from his plate or elsewhere came to epitomize, to characterize *en miniature*, so to speak, the land, the landscape, the region calling the young man home.

Ah, how his thoughts had drifted as he lay there remembering his dead brother. What counted, and what had to be reported on, was this above all: during the month in the foreign land, with him, his older brother, thanks to the expedition the two of them undertook, and altogether, Hans found his way to—what was it called?—a new life. He'd no sooner arrived for their first time together after many years, than it became obvious: the two of them didn't need to make peace. Even before that, despite all the insults, curses, and hateful comments they'd hurled at each other, despite their laughing at each other and refusing to meet each other's eyes, making peace later would hardly have occurred to them—not because it seemed impossible but because even then, including and specifically in the moments when both of them flew off the handle, along with or beneath the fraternal strife, the family conflict, outside of and within it, or somewhere, what mattered wasn't the yelling, the horrific posturing, the pseudo-enmity, the phony war, but, on the contrary, something serious, something real taking place, which didn't call for reconciliation. Away with pseudo-truces. Reconciliation as a concept: the phoniest thing of all?

Something else: the "healed patient," as he called himself, didn't fully participate in the expedition. That had as much to do with the nature of the expedition as with his own disposition, and not only his present disposition. The fact that he almost never asked questions might be attributable to the family and clan tradition. Yet from early on he'd also never had questions of any sort or carried a question around inside him like a pregnancy. Trailing his brother as the older man eagerly headed off on a promising wrong track, Hans would wait in silence, neither patiently nor impatiently, whenever Gregor stopped to record this or that fruit of roaming hither and yon and—O brave new geometries!—make sketches. Then he would follow Gregor to the next trigonometric point, Gregor's chosen non-destination, where they would pause temporarily after cutting across a field or steppe to reach it: an imaginary crossroads, from which, according to the older brother's decree, six roads branched off, each of the six promising additional fruitful opportunities for going astray.

"Trailing"? When a third person, a rarity, crossed their wrong track—it was always a single individual, whereas the two of them were plural, a duo—it could happen that this person took the younger man for the boss, not only because he was taller, and took the one tramping ahead for his aging scout or sherpa. That impression was reinforced by the gray in Gregor's hair and the furrows in a face bronzed like that of a mountaineer, whereas the one following in his footsteps (his legs so long that one of his steps equaled two of his brother's) met the description of a quintessential paleface—not typical of someone working in the building trades, the profession Hans hadn't been practicing during the period when he'd been loafing around and becoming a night person. And the difference between the two most noticeable to the observer: the one in front carried a pack, his back bent not only from age, while the one behind had his hands free, and strolled along with his head held high. But a few glances later, if our observer happened to still be in the mood for such, this unambiguous difference suddenly became ambiguous? No, indecipherable. For how could the man in front be merely a "porter" when his eyes, ears, and nostrils, as well as his fingertips, were responding to the multitude of occurrences on his wrong tracks and his lips were silently spelling out all the impressions his senses picked up? And how could the expedition leader be someone who, out of homesickness or hunger for "proper" foods and thirst for beverages that "hit the spot," seemed to have neither eyes nor appreciation for anything in this foreign land, for anything at all, from here to the horizon?

Senseless questions—the wrong ones. My third person: how could you know?

The only unambiguous part: as their joint undertaking progressed, the older one ascribed a lack of enthusiasm to the younger one, and not only in connection with the expedition in particular. But that he was clearly mistaken in this reproach, which, by the way, remained unspoken, would become evident on their last evening together, before the young man left for home.

True, there'd been plenty of evidence in the previous weeks to invalidate the older brother's assumption. More and more often, from day to day, Hans had jumped in, silently and without being asked, to help his brother in unobtrusive ways. "Jumped"? Could such a thing go unnoticed? Yes, it could.

And did Gregor really need someone to help him? He did—though he wasn't aware that was the case. Not that he was exceptionally inept, but he'd always been unusually slow when it came to everyday tasks, and if others were around, they never failed to lend a hand. He'd resisted being helped, however. Family members described how, even as a child, whenever another child wanted to help with something, Gregor would push the would-be helper away, sometimes yelling bloody murder. Later he learned to control such outbursts, but at least in the eyes of those around him who saw the need, he would fumble and bumble, making a hash of a task, and the closer they got to taking over, the more hopelessly clumsy he appeared, incompetence personified. "If I'd been by myself, with no one watching, I would've dealt with my snarls and tangles in peace, though maybe more slowly than you speed demons, because I relished taking my time."

Wasn't it true in general that with others watching he was at risk of losing his unique sense of time? And also true that his brother, whom he'd reproached initially for never watching him—not even looking at him, constantly looking past him or at most glancing at him out of the corner of his eye—embodied an inconspicuous form of helpfulness, which remained inconspicuous even when the situation got "serious"? Yes, that was it. And that kind of natural helpfulness the older brother allowed and came to value more and more as the month spent on their two-man expedition progressed, also because, each time, he realized only in retrospect that the younger man had jumped in to help, and in what way.

Gregor and Hans marked Hans's departure solemnly, also celebrating, without mentioning it, their finding each other again after all those years of estrangement, including those in Hans's childhood when the older one had been infuriatingly overconcerned about the other. Supper in a booth in a restaurant located on the bay across from the airfield where the young man would take off for home the following day. There Brother Hans ate fresh fish for the first time, his eyes laughing at Brother Gregor. And once he'd drunk—after a month without alcohol—his "well-deserved" glass of beer, he tried wine for the first time, puckering up not just his mouth but his whole face after the first sip, though by the third sip he was involuntarily savoring the aftertaste.

In their booth, dimly lit at the beginning but, as the evening wore on, glowing more and more brightly, in the bayside restaurant on a remote continent—"remote" in reference to where?—it happened that, toward midnight, the younger brother all of a sudden pulled out of his pocket a carefully folded piece of tear-resistant paper, the kind on which construction drawings used to be made, unfolded it solemnly, and stuck it under his brother's nose in the light of the table lamp.

In fact, it was a construction plan. And it had been drawn not by an architect or a contractor but by him, the journeyman builder who'd completed his training barely two years earlier. The plan showed the house he'd already been dreaming of during his apprenticeship, seeing himself living there someday with a wife and child, and for the rest of his life. Except that the drawing made do without details or extravagant amenities, unlike those one would see in the blueprint for a so-called dream house. If the older brother recalled correctly, the plan offered no specific features, didn't even hint at them, whether in writing or sketched. There was no "bath" or "bathroom" among the four or five rooms at least identified in the house—a "work" or "family" room, a "living" or "evening" room (also for the night?), a "child's room," and a surprisingly wide "hallway" leading diagonally from the front door, as wide as a portal, to the "kitchen" in the back, with one or two rooms opening off it at intervals, not labeled, their purposes unspecified. All this could be seen on the rather small sheet of paper, hastily sketched. But how straight all the lines were, though unmistakably drawn freehand, each in one firm stroke! And the thick black-crayoned half circle representing the arched entry to the single-story house (also without a cellar?): perfectly rounded, strikingly so, impossible to achieve with any tool, and establishing a rhythm that continued from line to line through the entire house, evocative of children's drawings, including their unfinished quality, their "lack of accuracy," and at the same time self-confident and proud.

At that late hour, the brothers ordered another bottle of wine. This was granted to them, although in their booth they were the restaurant's last guests, also last guests different from the usual ones, simply in the way they treated each other. Ships, festively illuminated, were still steaming into the bay, and each time the two of them looked out over the water, they felt as if the restaurant were moving, too, just as looking out from a train standing on the tracks at a train passing alongside creates the illusion of motion, and the brothers had that sensation at the same moment that they looked at the ships in the distance, and thus both felt they were moving during that hour, not into the bay but in the opposite direction, out to sea.

During that night at the window from which they could look out over the bay, the older brother also experienced the younger man as impassioned, and open as never before. Gregor couldn't recall a moment when he'd seen Hans show joy—he'd been joyless even as a child. But now: what joy he found in his older brother, in the world around him, and especially in himself.

This night saw another legend added to the stock of family and clan lore. And Hans was the one who created it, with his older brother as his willing accomplice at first and then his earnest co-creator. And the legend went this way: Whatever the "family" or the "clan" might say, our house, the house of our parents, our grandparents, and so forth, going way, way back, the house of our children and children's children, is a house in another sense—"the House of XY" (insert house name). We form a "lineage." Possibly even a "royal" one? Yes, indeed, a royal one! Or perhaps more likely an anti-royal one? Anti-kings in the sense of anti-popes. No idea what an anti-pope is, but anti-kings certainly in a different sense. In what sense, dear brother? A branch line, a distant one, dismissed as illegitimate, but actually in existence before the main lineage, which originally consisted only of a branch of a branch, except that we, our house, our lineage, in the course of the centuries never got its turn, and the one time we tried to assert it—we? our ancestors—we!—tried—what? to mount the throne? yes, to mount the throne!—the ancestor who tried it must have lost life and limb, and our lineage, which was banished to the ends of the earth, was downgraded to a mere clan in the best of cases. To wit, our father, as before him our grandfather: a clan of cottagers and small farmers—but at least farmers!—yet usually dodgy somehow, if not, now and then over the years, even violent, murderous, prone to strike out on the slightest pretext, also with an unusual number, even for a clan of unappreciated folk, of vagabonds, petty thieves, runaways, head-for-the-hillers, skedaddlers—yes, one skedaddler from the royal house on the heels of another!—or, on the contrary, a clan of couch potatoes, nook-and-cranny crouchers, shithouse stowaways, idiot-box starers and house posts—ah, that beautiful old term for our family idiots who from birth to death leaned, as stiff as boards, against the walls of the house! And then, finally, guys like me and you, the worst of the whole clan, with the royal patent in a back pocket like me or tucked into a breast pocket like you, my Lord Brother—right. SIRE: we two feel we're better than if we had a crown on our heads, which may be acceptable for me, once voted the best football goalie in the district league, second-lowest class, but not for you, the self-appointed hero of escapes into those threadbare one-man expeditions of yours.

That's all well and good. But is that the sum total of what you're aiming for with your fantasies of royal birth? Or do you dream of someday seeing one of your future children or children's children elevated to a throne of some kind?

I'm not aiming for anything, Brother, anything at all! I know you've never thought much of people who indulge in fantasizing, if you haven't rejected fantasy altogether. Or maybe you're afraid of it, especially your own? I, on the other hand, thrive on fantasizing. It fits my reality, as does the idea of our royal blood. I've always thrived on it, even if I hardly ever mentioned it, and certainly not to you. Do you know what I sometimes called you in my mind? "One-Eye," or "Old One-Eye." And you know that name also comes from something other than your loss of one eye that time you were sick as a child? And do you also know why I'm finally able to tell you this tonight? Because after tonight I'll never call you that again, not even more secretly than secretly. No more "Brother One-Eye."

Their last shared moments the next day, at the airport on the third or fifth continent from the vantage point of Europe—also the last moment when a member of the small family, "lineage" or not, laid eyes on what was then its youngest offspring. Looking back now, the older brother felt as if in that moment he'd already been in the presence of the future Foreign Legionnaire, his pupils motionless, slightly off-center. Yet once he got home Hans intended to get a regular job again, which in fact he did—"a new life"—"happy about it," since in the meantime his professional association had certified him as a journeyman builder, "pissing on the wet concrete with a bottle of beer in hand, but only after work was over for the day," convinced it was right for him. A year later, however, "Greetings from the Foreign Legion." And a year after that he showed up for his older brother once more, this time on the screen of his pocket telephone, merely shrugging when asked whether, as a legionnaire, he'd been involved in any battles, punitive expeditions (see "expedition"), or the like, and, in an involuntary response to the next question, only showed his face, the sound muted, rolling his eyes up at a tropical sky of some sort outside the frame, those eyes frozen in a cramp that didn't release them for a long, long time.

ON THE LAST GUEST: A BALLAD

The night was still very dark, but already the first bird could be heard, known in that region as the "lone whistler," though its song sounded less like whistling than like an almost inaudible one-syllable chirping from an unspecified location, a wondrously delicate sound, and only then did sleep come to the weary cross-continental traveler in his childhood bedroom, a dreamless sleep, or at least one on which dreams left no imprint.

It was early afternoon when he woke up, a waking more gentle than gentle, at least when he first opened his eyes in the triangular space under the roof—a sensation of having been prodded by something. In spite of the noises making their way into his room from far off in the great agglomeration, workday noises for the most part, with the early-fall sun high in the curtainless window, it felt like a Sunday to him, again at least during the first minutes between waking and sleeping, and without having anything particular in mind, as if steered remotely, he took the few steps to the armoire, the only piece of furniture aside from the bed and the table and chair, and took out the one somewhat dressy garment, his well-worn and reliably moth-hole-free Sunday suit (thank you, Mother dear), put it on with slow, deliberate ceremony, and inspected himself from all sides in the imaginary mirror.

He'd been careful while carrying out these operations to make no noise. Complete absence of sound, if possible. And he continued the effort as he opened the skylight, which his considerate mother—or perhaps his sister?—had closed while he was sound asleep. There was the apple tree in the backyard, with the play of sun, shade, and wind in its still-dense foliage creating the image of a figure secretly scrambling up the trunk—an apple thief? And, facing it from across the way at the open window, he suddenly found himself looking forward to winter and the bare trees, longed to see even the evergreens, which weighed on his heart, stripped bare. Ah, the chill of winter mornings that would let me see my breath in a cloud, banishing my nightmares, as I stood here at the window. Clouds of breath in the tropics? Not going to happen, not there. Or maybe after all?

No noise, not a sound elsewhere in the house, and not coming from the few outbuildings on the property that had survived through the decades, including from the tiny chicken coop. Had the weasel come overnight? Did urban weasels exist, perhaps actual big-city ones?

In fact, he didn't question the silence in the house below: he was sure they were there, his few relatives, his father, mother, and sister, each occupied as usual during the day, and if one of them made any noise, it was so muffled that it didn't find its way from the rooms, hallways, and workshop to him upstairs.

After he'd transferred anything he'd need for the day from his traveling clothes to his Sunday suit, leaving behind all his other belongings, including his duffel bag, he made his way slowly, slowly down the stairs. No need to tiptoe to avoid making noise; from early childhood and childhood games, he remembered exactly which steps, when he went up and down, creaked most noticeably. And it was almost the same to this day, of that he was certain: If anything, the creaking of a particular step would be gone. Or a little louder? No, quieter.

Having finally reached the front hall on the ground floor, after an interval that seemed quite long to him—a quarter of an hour? if not half an hour?—he heard from the other side of the door under the stairs, which opened into the former toolshed, now his sister's realm, the voice of a child. That has to be my chubby, Buddha-bellied future godchild. Yes, our only progeny till now—and may it remain that way!—is just waking up from his midday nap. He's lying in there alone, the little boy, without curly hair, unlike the Baby Jesus in the Christmas carol, almost without hair at all, and chortling and chattering away, filling the lovely still air as only a well-nourished infant, pleased with himself and the world, can. How devilishly contented that little guy seemed last night.

And already his plan of leaving the house was postponed, as, almost reflexively, his hand pressed the latch of the door under the stairs—more soundlessly, if possible, than if the action had been intentional—and the chosen godfather found himself in the presence of the godson-to-be. He wasn't lying in his crib, however, but sitting up, swaying slightly, whether because he had just sat up, still drunk with sleep, or because he hadn't mastered sitting up yet, or, God forbid, never would.

But what was this? The child, in the dim light—a holdover from the room's former function as a storage area—with only a pair of large eyes visible through the crib's bars, seemed oblivious to him at first. And that was no illusion. Maybe the infant did see the other person standing one or two paces away but looked right past him, didn't register him; his mother's brother simply didn't exist for him. And if the little fellow, broader than he was tall, now stopped chattering, that surely had nothing to do with the massive figure trying to catch his eye. Then what did it mean? Don't know. Whatever the case: no longer vocalizing but continuing to sit, holding on to the bars, the child threw his head back, and with his eyes, unblinking, fixed on the ceiling, suddenly ("suddenly" again), a good while later, burst out laughing, the laughter having clearly built up gradually during his previous silence, expressing enthusiasm such as could come only from a little human who'd been expelled from his mother's womb into the outer world only the day before, so to speak, laughter at nothing at all, a hairline crack in the ceiling, a spot the size of a fingernail up there where the plaster had peeled. Nothing worth mentioning?

"Listen up, you little good-for-nothing," the man began, scolding his godson-to-be after taking a step toward the crib and going down on his knees, eye to eye with the child, whose laughter even before this, as often happens with babies, had slipped into an almost inaudible whining. And now the child finally noticed the grown-up and took him in, despite how softly he was speaking, almost in a whisper, or precisely for that reason? No more whining; the mini-embodiment of attentiveness. Was this little person hanging on the scolder's words? Indeed he was, and more and more so in the course of the stream of invective that followed, as the whispering eventually became hoarse. It seemed as if the child were reading the litany from the grown-up's lips. Yes, "reading"; that was how contagiously the whispered rhythm communicated itself to him—not the words he was hearing—and caused the child's head to bob along and his lips to move for moments in harmony with the harsh words being hissed into his face, barely a hand's breadth away. And it was unmistakable that the baby enjoyed picking up the rhythm of the syllables spewing from the mouth of the stranger, that he took it for a game, a joke, in which he was now playing along. And the sparse strands of hair on his strangely large baby's head whipped back and forth, and there was a pulsing in the spot on his skull, round as a coin, protected not by bone but only by the skin covering it, which wouldn't "harden" until the following year.

And this spot, the fontanel, pulsed and pulsed, not yet in response to "You good-for-nothing" but thanks to several more invectives: for instance, "Wolf's child with milk teeth!," "Room for three tax collectors!," "Member of the Radebeul, Zamora, Toledo, and Oberlaar Church Tower Sparrows choirs!," "Tom Thumb stinking like ten manure-spreaders!," "Spitting image of your unknown father!," "Food snatcher!," "Mini-Moses swimming in your own piss!," "Fart-Kaspar!," "Pear-cider slurper!," "Snot-bell ringer," "Accountant!," "Ne'er-do-well with a snow-white loser's ass!," "Merry-go-round owner's sidekick!," "Apron chaser running home to Mama's apron strings!," "Oh, you, you little guy, my hope as the last in our line, as the last thing!"

And the child was so tickled by playing along that his face didn't just light up with laughter; he literally shouted with glee—yes, glee—and then he reached out his arms to the stranger to be lifted out of the crib, or just lifted closer to the ceiling. But even now Gregor couldn't overcome his squeamishness about touching a child, and that wouldn't change. Baptism, godfather duties: not happening unless the child in his arms was so thickly swaddled that nothing from his little body would put his "one-man expeditions" in jeopardy. But what was going on? All the children through the years, the little and even more the littlest ones, more plainly than the older ones, had shied away at the sight of his blind eye—and this one hadn't noticed it?

He had to get away. Out the door—not the front, the back one—and away, away from the house through the door in the wall that enclosed the backyard. One final look over his shoulder at the crib: the child sitting there just as when he'd entered, not looking at him, but now he wasn't looking in any direction, was playing with a stuffed animal, a bunny, and, what do you know, it was a real rabbit, a live one, which had been sleeping earlier or hiding and now let the child pull its ears, pretended to hop away, and came right back.

No glance over his shoulder, however, as he made his way through the yard and slipped out through the door in the wall. If he'd been observed escaping, those in the house wouldn't have been surprised, for they thought or believed they knew the son's and brother's proclivities and idiosyncrasies from his previous "home leaves." "That's just how he is!" the mother would have said to the sister, or more likely the other way around, the sister to the mother, because Sophie had always fancied herself Gregor's confidante, his only one.

As he did every year on the day after his arrival, he set out for the family orchard, hardly tended anymore, as had long been the case, and tended less every year, which meant it would have shrunk by one tree or more, and whereas it had originally been a bright, airy enclosure, surrounded by open fields on all sides, it was now surrounded or even hemmed in, though at a slight distance, by rather modest industrial complexes and commercial facilities, most of them single-story.

The orchard, not to be confused with today's single-crop plantations, had been established at least a century earlier, the work of one member of the family—a "Gregor," like every firstborn. They hadn't begun keeping track until later, with the result that the orchard-Gregor was called "the third," though he might have been god knows which one in the succession. And me? Gregor the Last?

The route to the orchard consisted of a succession of paths: first a paved road, then sand-and-gravel paths, widened on each side to accommodate trucks, with tar added only to fill the numerous potholes. The network followed quite faithfully the course of the former dirt roads between and across fields and through wooded areas, including the ditches alongside that still had water in them, one of which, in a particularly flat stretch, widened into a meandering brook, but a bit farther on, in the midst of the thickly settled agglomeration that had sprung up suddenly next to the semi-no-man's-land, it had been diverted, maybe as much as decades ago, to flow under the pavement, transformed into a canal, out of sight and likewise out of earshot, other than on a soundless night after a downpour.

What now took him by surprise: after the first bend on the road to the orchard, a rushing sound at odds with an urban environment and the peripheries solidifying on all its borders. The roaring, even rushing, came from the country brook formerly banished underground and now rerouted into daylight. But no: it had sounded that way for only a moment, not like the rushing of the long-ago brook. A few steps farther on—if only it had been the distance traversed by a real arrow at least, instead of a dart—the brook disappeared again, without a peep, far below the street; its brief appearance had been engineered as an enhancement to the streetscape, accompanied by the particular rushing, not monotonous in the slightest but many-voiced, of the actual, authentic brook, its flow intensified by the hydraulics or such created by blocks of real granite around and over which the water swirled, generating a pounding or drumming, voices telling you something you've forgotten, something that since the loss of your eye you've not wanted to hear, have kept at arm's length. A tableau, merely decorative, including the flakes of mica: how they glitter and sparkle in your granite! Yes, decorative and attractive, no doubt. But does attractiveness like that mean nothing? If I'd been you, I'd have gone so far as to drink that water.

In recent years, he'd already been struck by all the unoccupied houses in the area, some half finished and rotting away, others, still inhabited on his previous visits, now not merely unoccupied but abandoned, deserted for good. Not a soul, let alone a couple, a family, or some other group, would ever move in and "reside" there. Yet these houses seemed perfectly sound, intact, needing only a few touches to be "move-in ready." Not a for-sale sign in sight, however. And apparently no heirs showing up either. And this time the untouched "estates" had been joined by one or more, like the one two blocks over, in the section that still belonged to his old neighborhood, by now less his than his parents'. Solid masonry construction, closed shutters, their paint colors still fresh, not a single crooked louver or rail on any of the shutters. Were they closed only temporarily, for a brief absence, or maybe just for this particular day?

Or against the glare of the sun? Closed forever, shut up tight! Yet, on the other hand, in perfect condition, and looking as if polished that very morning: the old brass plaque to the right of the front door, "Mason Contractor," along with the surname of the father and son still offering their expert workmanship, generation after generation.

He'd paused there, taking in the tiny front garden, which provided the only unmistakable sign that everything was "over and done with." Overgrown vegetation, shoulder-high or taller, unidentifiable, consisting mostly of scraggly yellowish stalks with bleached remnants of shriveled empty seedpods on top: weeds filling the entire garden. *I see something you don't see!* No, I saw it long before you: the couple of rosebushes up against the house, in full bloom. But they're destined to be swallowed up in a week at most by the weeds, the last touch on the image of "over and done with." *Good heavens, I see something else you don't see.* And what do you see, for god's sake, that apparently escapes me? *First of all, please, that's enough about "weeds"—don't use that word, or any words like that. And these thousands, these thousand and one stalks, aren't "scraggly"; they're actually "slender" and "flexible," and those aren't "pods" on top but "blossoms," whorl upon whorl of blossoms, a thousand and one times more delicate than the roses. And, ah, I see something else you don't see: clustered on the blossoms or blooming heads of your weeds, a whole colony of late-summer bees. And in the roses? Not a bee. Oh, yes, the weed blossoms are of a color you've never run into anywhere.* The name of that color? *Hasn't been invented yet.* You and your incessant fantasizing. *Yes, and again I see what you don't see: the roses aren't in any danger of being swallowed up or choked; instead, they've freed themselves of their own accord, if not torn themselves away, from their trellis, their trellis cage, their trellis cage on the wall of the abandoned house, and now they're standing, held up by the late-summer wind, looking down on that front garden, hardly wider than a person's forearm, still occupied by the overgrown vegetation, facing down the nameless crowd. And how they stand tall, my weed stalks. And how the stalks of your roses bob up and down, back and forth, bowing awkwardly, to salute my weeds.* And in a week, when the two species, defying all precautions, have grown together and crossed—the roses and the nameless plants—what will a cross like that look like? *Yes, like what?* Which face will it have? *Yes, which?*

It was also remarkable to see how, in one year's time, the spaces once cultivated but now lying fallow, along with the abandoned houses, seemed to have multiplied, apparently unusable forever. "No-man's-land" was the right term for such vacant lots, often hardly as big as the penalty box on a football pitch—tundra-like—inhospitable, empty, but spared the heaps of trash accumulating elsewhere. But was that term still appropriate?

Be that as it may: On his way to the orchard, such spots, in contrast to the abandoned houses, were usually farther from the road and not visible from there, tucked away in the hinterland. But he sensed their presence nonetheless and made a detour to some of them, drawn to them as someone with a professional obligation to them, and each time it seemed to him as if the empty lot came to meet him. Nothing like a penalty box.

True enough, there were various kinds of obligation, and he knew that the kind he viewed as ideal and had taken the greatest pleasure in fulfilling could change in a flash into an annoyance. What was concerning and even dangerous wasn't pretending to remain committed but, rather, continuing to do his duty mechanically. And what was the danger? That he, once he lost his gusto for fulfilling an obligation—see the "joyful walker" in one of the apostles' epistles—and carrying on mechanically, might come to see himself as an automaton, not only partially, in individual or partial actions, but as an automaton through and through, in his entire existence. And that in gaining such an awareness, instead of being mercifully canceled out, as a person devoid of feeling, he would experience intense pain. Awareness of pain? No, pain as awareness, the most acute pain of all.

But this danger, if it had threatened him repeatedly in the course of his life, sometimes from close up, sometimes from afar, and occasionally seeming to have been banished forever—which made it especially important to be watchful, but how?—had passed him by every time. And at this particular moment, during these days at home, it was crucial not to do anything to provoke that danger! Or maybe it was important after all to provoke danger during this week, but of a different kind.

Accordingly, he forbade himself to take those detours to the no-man's-patches, staying on course to the orchard instead, or what might be left of it. He did continue to allow himself to go cross-lots occasionally, "as in the old days": that, too, a source of pleasure, but one that had nothing to do with fulfilling an obligation. But he further forbade himself running, and adopted this as a rule for the coming days. Nothing but walking, not a single rapid step, no matter what! Yet: Now! Will you look at that? In the pre-autumnal blue sky, among all the usual contrails, two of "the third sort": one in the shape of a mighty bow, stretched tight; the other as the arrow, its tip resting on the bowstring, ready to be released. How I loved playing bow-and-arrow as a child, and what a good shot I was with my one eye, unmatched by any of the other players, yet I can't recall any target other than the poster with the monthly movie schedule pasted on the barn wall. Yes, none of you were good enough shots for me, including you. But what a catcher you were, and not only of balls—simply phenomenal!

The hollow with the orchard: was it considered part of the New Town, or was it assigned to the outskirts? But did all the new towns established over the last few decades, under a comprehensive urban expansion plan, even have such a thing as outskirts? Questions to be answered by someone else, someone in authority. At any rate, as he got closer, he was greeted by various local residents as an old friend, while he merely pretended to recognize them. "It's been so long!" "Yes, haven't seen you in ages!" And then experiences they'd supposedly shared long ago were recounted, things of which the homecomer had not the slightest memory, things he was sure he'd never participated in. But that was fine: how congenial, how heartwarming these false memories were! *Why "false"? Why don't you want to own them?*

What occurred to him later, as he was going downhill, step by step, to the oval-shaped orchard, was a feature he'd observed in all the people who'd recognized him on that final stretch, whether actually or mistaking him for someone else. As different from one another as people could be, they were all somehow out of the ordinary, each in his or her own way. Furthermore, they all had a burden to bear, and not only since that day or the one before. They had sorrow, unmitigated sorrow; they were in mourning for something or other; they had a disability, whether visible or not, were haunted—day in, day out—by fear of death. If they thought they recognized him, for a moment—and what a moment!—they were relieved of their fear; and in one way or another—back to "abstraction"—they all, in contrast to ordinary folk, had either too little or too much of something, and their out-of-the-ordinariness was their eternal woe, resembling, only in those few exceptional moments, a dance, but what a dance! "Hey there, my people!": That was him, still on his way into the hollow.

One reason it was taking him so long: he was following paths worn into the hillside by cattle ages ago, when the area was still pastured, paths not just still visible today but also still walkable. These paths didn't lead steeply downhill; rather, they ran horizontally along the slope, in almost parallel serpentines, which only in the turns or switchbacks went one hoof-step lower. And, following the cows and oxen of yore, he worked his way down the hundreds of serpentines, changing direction when they did, not skipping a single one—which would have been easy, because the paths were quite close to one another. The cattle grazing there hadn't skipped any paths either. Or perhaps some had, after all. The calves? Who knows? And the bulls? No, not them; if they were put out to pasture at all, it would have been somewhere else entirely.

At the bottom of the hollow it seemed as if the sun was about to set. In contrast to earlier that day, the newly arrived visitor burst out, "Not now! It's too early! Don't go!" And the sun stayed; its setting had been a false alarm. The trees stood there clearly lit, as if by spotlights, from above as well as from below. "Fruit season." But no fruit to be seen. In the foliage, sparse for this time of year, a round apple, or a pear shape among the limp leaves, would have been instantly noticeable. The previous year, at least the quince sapling way in the back of the oval had borne fruit, or, in the idiom of this once productive fruit-growing area, they would have said, "It was bearing, the tree, it's bearing, it will have borne."

A wind gust then, a downdraft such as had occurred sometimes, though rarely, in the wind-shielded hollow. "After all!" All the more tangible, then, the subsequent absence of wind. In the crown of the one tree that, unlike the others, was almost dense with green leaves, there was now a cracking sound—no, a sizzling; no, a rustling; no, a rumbling; no, no, a knocking—nonsense, a sound for which no word existed, or several, many, infinitely many, and then that's enough stretching, estimating distances, testing the takeoff! And suddenly there was a pounding, a crash, a crashing through the whole tree, the smashing from limb to limb of something heavy falling toward the ground: an apple after all, a single one, one of a kind, letting go of its twig, starting to fall, catapulting in stages down through the tree, and now, almost as big as a turnip, with red-and-white stripes, coming to rest in the orchard grass with its stem sticking straight up? More nonsense: that was your imagination, pure and simple; that happened long ago; that was how you once heard an apple fall to the ground. Your orchard, the family orchards: beyond saving.

As he pictured it—you know how that is?—he had an ax and a saw at hand and was already hacking away, already sawing at the nearest half- or completely dead tree in his line of sight, until it cracked and fell on the dry grass, actually more moss and lichen than grass. The saw had gone through too fast. No, in this case imagination wasn't enough; he would need a real saw if he wanted to put an end, or at least the beginning of an end, to our orchard.

And then a real saw turned up, in what remained of the wooden shed, now overgrown with thistles and brambles, that had once been a feature of the orchard, on whose edge another of the no-man's-patches had formed long ago, the smallest of all on this day, with the industrial and commercial complexes beyond it, their backs to the orchard. And the saw's teeth were so rusty that they couldn't eat through the trunk of the actual fruit tree, and it wasn't only the fault of the teeth: the tree, although dead or dying, was very different from the one in his imagination.

But something had to be done. Our orchard, a hopeless ruin, had to disappear from the face of the earth, and the last of all the Gregors in our family had to give the signal for that, now, at once. And, as would be recorded by him in the chronicle of what ensued, having tossed away the useless saw after countless attempts, he stormed up the hill and across the plateau to the expanse of commercial buildings, where he borrowed a chain saw from a security guard, who was happy to recognize him, by the way, from somewhere or other, and stormed back down into the hollow, where etc., etc.

What he didn't take into account: when pelting up the hill, he'd paid no mind to the paths worn by the cattle's hoofs that he'd followed so conscientiously, step by step, on his original descent; now he completely disregarded the time-honored model of moving through space, turn after turn after turn, or was simply blind to it.

And there was something else missing from his chronicle, something he'd overlooked, however intently he'd focused on his "chronicler's duty." He felt its absence only later, when the chronicle was already finished, at least in his mind—not yet written but impossible to add to, even to correct, and, besides, there was no longer time or space for that. But for here and now: while poking around for the rusty saw in the tumbledown orchard shed, he'd come upon something among, next to, and behind the brambles and the tangle of vines, something that appeared to him only later, particularly vivid as an afterimage, and that was the wild-apple sapling in the underbrush, actually a mere bush, or a bush amid brush, but covered with fruit, more fruit than leaves, the wild apples teeny-tiny, and more green than yellow or red. Evergreen. Due to be ripe on the Greek calends, or on the Emperor's Birthday. One bite: so tart it makes your asshole contract till it's sealed tight. Here's wishing the whole world a bite like that!

And what happened next? I returned the chain saw to my friend the security guard. Then I made my way to the last streetcar stop. Sitting on the bench outside the nearby refreshment stand, I ate a sandwich. The dog who lay down at my feet was much smaller than the one from the previous day, but it was the same dog. Then I took Line Such-and-such back and forth through the New Town. At the multiplex, twenty-eight screening rooms in a building shaped like an enormous blimp, I got off and took in a movie, the title and plot of which I've forgotten.

Here's what he did recall from that late afternoon, before and during the movie: All of a sudden, the light became unbearable, not only when he looked up at the sky, but also when he looked down at the ground, at the reddish-yellow clay and the black ribbons of tar on the gray asphalt, at the sewer grates, reflecting the sun, low in the sky, in a glaring, painful, checkered pattern. Now all he could think of was getting indoors—quick,

quick—into any one of the twenty-eight theaters that would shield him from all that light in the open sky, and it didn't matter which movie was playing. During the screening, every time he glanced over his shoulder from his seat in one of the front rows at the sparse audience, he could make out a single face here and there, all the more visible in the dark. One couple, merely sensed in the background, was the exception. The others, all there by themselves, seemed advanced in years, and were apparently of the same age and as like as peas in a pod (no, not peas), and the lighting on the screen, changing from one frame to the next, flickered on the faces, all equally expressionless, of these viewers, who looked absent from themselves. And the flickering light appeared as a new kind of eyelash flutter, a new kind of blink.

And there was something else he wouldn't forget from that hour in the movie theater—or at least not soon—though he might have wished to forget it—or maybe not, after all: how, in the middle of the film, when the two main characters, a man and a woman, a woman and a man, for the third or fourth time in the course of the story, begin, with appropriate background music, to rip off each other's clothes, the woman the man's and the man the woman's, both of them breathing faster, and the man in the man's role and the woman in the woman's role accompanied by the musical scales, one rising, the other descending, associated in such a situation with the two sexes (ideally as well as in reality the most serious of situations—which here, before us audience members, horror of horrors, had to be perverted into its opposite)—so when the actor and the actress, the actress and actor, again began to humiliate themselves and me along with them, legitimated by the declaration, a declaration with the force of a legal decision, that this sort of thing was a component, an indispensable component, of their profession, and a refusal to participate in it would be deemed unprofessional—at that moment, the humiliated and offended viewer, who, upon seeing such scenes the first few times, had merely, in no matter what part of the world he found himself, turned his eyes away from the images and sounds on the screen to the most imageless corner of the theater, now stood—no, jumped—up from the seat in movie-theater darkness that had been so welcome to him on this particular day, gave the seat a kick, and shouted—in reality just muttered, though he heard it in his head as shouting—"No more movies! Down with movies that violate the audience's rights. So this crap is supposed to come along with democracy? Down with democracy, away with everything-goes democracies, in the name of the people. Which people? Where are you, people? Let's have a dictatorship, a new kind, one that bans what deserves to be banned. *Vita nuova!*" And already he was out the door, though he first stumbled through the wrong one. And not one member of the audience looked away from the screen while I was proclaiming my new society. With the swelling wailing, screeching, panting, and moaning above their heads, they hadn't taken in a single word of my proclamation, and my stomping and then striding away from the world stage also went unnoticed.

In the meantime, the sun had set, this time for real, and an early dusk seemed to veil the air close to the ground, which had the effect of intensifying the outlines of every object and everything taking place there. Glancing up at the sky, he saw the multiplex blimp going up in flames, tipping out of its moorings, and crashing to the ground.

In an annex to the shopping center, he purchased a pair of sunglasses, the darkest ones in the shop, which were still by no means dark enough, though he'd tried on pair after pair. He had no trouble making out clearly, with his one eye, anything around him, whether in motion or motionless—things in motion or moving actually clearer than motionless ones—and objects and actions seen out of the corner of his eye at least as clear as those seen head-on. Over the decades, he'd grown used to missing one eye, or so he imagined. With my one intact eye, and not just with its outer but—picture this!—also its inner corner, the one by my nose, I can by now look out over my nose and take in every situation and anything happening around me, and all without needing to turn my head—unlike owls, with their cornerless eyes!

Behind his dark glasses, he now had a visual field superior to that of many people with two good eyes in broadest daylight. Mightn't these glasses, so funereally black and, moreover, Ray-Ban–like, enormously large, be mistaken for a blind person's? Yes, possibly, but only at first glance, and only if the glance took in nothing but the glasses, not their wearer. The way he walks bears no resemblance to the gait of a blind person, a "visually impaired" person, a "*mal voyant.*" *So tell me: how does he walk?* Well, he no longer walks as he once did, in long, theatrical steps, a stride bespeaking power, the stride of the last in his line. *So how does he walk now?* In this second dusk, a deep one, in this prelude to night, he walks as Gregor, not as "the last" (in quotation marks: "the Last"?), but, rather, without any number, as "*der Gregor,*" a name that in translation means . . . *From what language?* From any language you please . . . Which suggests, first of all, "I was awakened," and then: "I woke up," and, furthermore, "I'm awake," and then "I keep watch," and then "I snap to attention," and, as a description of a person, "the watchful one," "the watchman," or "the person on watch." *But how does a person like that, a person on watch, walk—walk and keep watch at the same time?* Yes, how?

It was assumed that during his week at home Gregor would at least turn up for supper at his parents' house on the street still designated by the sign on the corner as "Garden Lane," even though all that remained of the once-continuous line of gardens planted with fruit trees and vegetables—never more than one (1) bed for flowers, "the flower bed"—was one, the "vestigial garden," as it were.

After nightfall, when the almost big-city-style streetlights came on all at once, extending to the most distant horizons, where they appeared very faint, he was drifting around in a section now incorporated into the New Town but once part of his old village. Every year more sections were added in this way as the agglomeration spread. What was going on? Drifting around like this had never been his thing, had it? But that's how it was: he was drifting around. Or how about this: he let himself be driven hither and yon, confident that, without having to search, he'd come upon a night-dark corner, whether one from before or a new one. There he'd take off his dark glasses, though only for a minute. But no such spot turned up. Wherever he roamed, brightness and more brightness. Why not duck into one of the bars, a "bistro," a "pub," a "cocktail lounge," where the lighting, seen from the outside, in contrast to the lighting on the streets, including the narrowest alleys, usually looked filtered, veiled somehow, the more so when the windows had no curtains? No, taverns, cafés, seedy bars, and the like had never appealed to him, Expedition Man, unless there was something to celebrate; see the description above of the bayside restaurant on the next-to-last continent from his birthplace. *But what was there to celebrate on an evening like this, and with whom? Tell me, with whom?*

To tell the truth, he felt drawn away from the streets, especially the quieter ones, which seemed all the more exposed to the harsh lighting; he felt drawn to that other kind of light. Because of the voices and music that found their way outside, reaching him as he drifted around? That may have been one attraction, but the one that counted was the different light. *And why didn't you let yourself be drawn in?* I hadn't reached that point yet. Instead, I turned in the opposite direction, toward

Garden Lane. No moon; only the Dog Star again. Also, not a breath of wind, let alone a buffeting night-wind. Where are you, late-summer storms, with real thunder and lightning? Is it already goodbye for now, till we meet again—not too soon—next year?

A glance from the street into the house, into the large family room (almost as big as a restaurant's dining room), revealed everything to be the same, aside from insignificant details, as when he'd arrived the night before. He hadn't handed out gifts to individual family members, only a couple for the house, like those he brought every year, picked up on an expedition or something, small items that took up hardly any room in his duffel bag. That was another unwritten law in the family: no personal gifts, only a few for the house. Incidentally, the night before he'd almost forgotten the usual domestic ceremony, and not until he picked up his bag around midnight to carry it up to his room under the eaves did he remember to hand over the gifts, something he usually took care of first thing upon arriving; but it wasn't the right moment, so he simply placed the gifts to the house, unceremoniously and wordlessly, on the table in the family room. Over his shoulder, he heard the comment, called after him or sung in unison by his mother and sister, "Gregor, who never forgets, Gregor, the watchman, thoughtful Gregor. But tonight Gregor the forgetful, the watchman asleep at his post, absentminded all evening!"

And now, the next evening: What had he brought to contribute to the evening meal? What had he picked or collected as he spent the livelong day drifting around on highways and byways, what ingredients, promising exotic tastes, had he tucked into the deep, wide pockets of his Sunday suit—"Look, Father!"—unfamiliar wondrous things? Nothing, nothing at all, his suit showing no signs of his having been engaged in anything productive for himself and the others. The creases in the trousers were crisp; the pocket square was as white as apple blossoms, if not quince blossoms; there was not the slightest snag in his trouser cuffs from the brambles along the edges of the old orchard. But now, look, in one cuff a single rowan berry, which fell out of your hand unnoticed, as sometimes happens with a coin or even a bead! This one berry as your contribution, no matter how bitter it tastes. And it's also supposed to be toxic. But if so, only slightly. And there's nothing more wholesome, more healthful, than a smidgen of poison, right?

That said, he was about to come home empty-handed, entirely out of character—his hands empty and, at the same time, as he involuntarily held them in front of him, so heavy suddenly that in that moment they dropped away from him, together with his arms, toward the ground. And being without arms was very different from having only one eye.

What cheered him, however, beside, behind, and beyond the situation, as he kept his eye on the remaining members of the clan there in the house, was a memory stemming from what had once been called a "genre picture." During his years as a student, at the end of every summer, after protracted farewells, he'd made his way on foot down country roads and across fields to the railroad station, almost half a day's hike away, to return to the university, where he had a job as an assistant in the geology department. (One could still get there on foot, walking through the agglomeration—if, for instance, the transport workers went on strike again.) Halfway to the station, he'd turned back—he no longer recalled whether he'd left something at home that he couldn't do without, or for some other reason. As he approached the outskirts of the village, he heard singing in the distance and recognized the voices, or, as he'd expressed it as a youth, was "forced to recognize them," from the first few notes, as those of his mother and his sister, one of whom was given to trilling, and the other of whom liked singing slightly off-key. What was new this time was a third voice chiming in, a male voice. Hardly possible that it could be his father's: Gregor had never in his life heard him sing, and he, the son, wasn't the only one who hadn't. How tentatively that man was singing, as if shyly—yes, singing shyly, and, instead of joining the other two, singing a separate part, adding an undertone, but a confident one, from which he refused to be diverted. And with the door in the garden wall already half open, it had dawned on Gregor that the third singer was the youngest, hardly past his change of voice, and seeming to incorporate that into his singing. How the three of them sat there, and are sitting, and will have been sitting, in the mid-September sun, on the patch of lawn that had always felt like an entire meadow, on a tablecloth or bedsheet, and how merry they were as they sat there, and how carefree, at leisure, how relieved to put those strenuous summer days with their "always serious" older son and brother behind them, free at last to live their lives without his judgmental eyes on them, and with the tears they'd wept that morning at his departure now dried, they no longer needed the sad songs, not usual in their area, songs of sorrow and mourning, that they'd sung to see him off to that unfamiliar place where his absence would make them miss him after a while, but where, god willing, he would stay for a good long time, postponing his visits and his presence here in the house, not merely for the summer but time and again!

The tableau now seen through the windows, two decades and more since the one on the lawn, differed from that one in many respects, yet also repeated it. The people, too, his father and mother, and his sister with the baby on her lap, whether they were expecting the son and brother for supper or not, were sufficient unto themselves and in good spirits—the best spirits imaginable, and that was evident even if not a sound reached him out there on Garden Lane, not even from the infant squirming on his mother's lap. No heads turning to the wall clock, no dealing of cards onto the table, no eyeing of fingertips on the table's edge. Whether talking or listening, they were fully present, and even when they all remained silent, they seemed focused on one another. At one point, a flurry of motion as the mother, who up to then had been perched on the edge of her seat as if poised to swing into action, dashed, like several women in one, out of the picture—i.e., toward the kitchen—and then came sashaying back, almost in square-dance steps, accompanying herself with the family laugh, overly loud, which for a moment could be heard out on the street—or was he merely imagining that?—and, whatever the case, caused him to burst out laughing. And then, hearing himself laugh, he realized that since he'd received the news of his brother's death his laugh had been so hearty, so uninhibited. Looking up, he saw that the welcome garland from the night before had disappeared from above the front door. He picked up his hat, which had fallen out of his hand, put it on, and went on his way, not caring in which direction, into the night.

During the pre-midnight hours, he was seen by one person or another crisscrossing that section of town. One time he was sitting on the bench in a bus shelter, using his checkered handkerchief to polish his sunglasses, and after putting them on he spread the handkerchief, large enough for two faces, over his face and chest. Then he was standing on a square ringed with plane trees, under the one tree the birds had chosen for sleeping, but most of them—no migratory ones still around—were so lively and noisy that it seemed he was standing there less to take in their pre-bedtime peeping and chirping than to let the sparrows, chickadees, and whatever other small birds were present "shit on him," as an eyewitness put it. He let one beggar kiss his hand and shooed the next one away—no, actually pushed him away—and it wouldn't have taken much for him to get into a scuffle with that one, something more typical of his brother, at least in his youth. Another time, and somewhere else entirely, this man, known earlier for being rather unapproachable, preoccupied with his own (unknown) problems, if not allergic to being spoken to, was observed on one of the streets still crowded with pedestrians at that late hour saying hello to people at random and being greeted in return, almost matter-of-factly by almost all of them, who apparently weren't even particularly surprised. And was it only thanks to the sunglasses that, to the astonishment of one chronicler or another of this first half of the night, not a few of the women he encountered, and especially the genuinely beautiful beauties, alas so rare, both accompanied and unaccompanied ones, appeared willing—to what?—willing, willing to continue the game, which, incidentally, hadn't even begun at that point? And then the one who remarked in passing, "You're headed in the wrong direction."

In one of the open shops or supermarkets he bought a toothbrush, in another a hat, in the next one shoelaces, in yet another a T-shirt imprinted with FADED GLORY, in yet another a map of the entire agglomeration, in the one after that a flashlight, and in the following a penknife, etc., etc.: just one thing, a single object, in each store, purchase after purchase. As if grounded in—no, drawn into—the goings-on—nothing special—into the human world, every time he stepped over the threshold, even a merely imaginary one—"merely"—of another establishment identified as a "market," however tiny, he pictured himself following an unwritten commandment: "Thou shalt buy something for me, you, him, her, us, today and every day!" And thus, during this half of the night, his purchases gave him the special good feeling of fulfilling a prayer.

That he then took a seat at the one unoccupied table in a sidewalk café had nothing to do with all that, however. Without warning, as almost always, he was hungry, and though he hadn't felt cold all night, he was hankering for something that would warm him up. At the table next to his was another person sitting by himself, of whom all he could make out in the again seemingly veiled light was that he was very old, an ancient. And how straight he sits there, how quietly, how . . . almost otherworldly. And then it was he who recognized the old man, not the other way around, as had been the case all day: That's him, no doubt about it, the priest who stepped down, the "Reverend Father," the onetime pastor of our now silent and scattered village congregation, the one who a decade ago had shed his heavy priestly vestments and exchanged them for civilian dress, so much lighter and airier. Just look at how straight he sits! "But later this week—or did I only dream this?—you'll have to put on those ornate trappings one last time, for one very last service. Do I have that right or not?"

The gentleman thus addressed, in an extra-loud voice, at first seemed not to have heard these words, or to have thought they weren't meant for him; he turned his head toward another table near his. But then, what felt like hours later, as if the message had gone halfway around the world before reaching him, he suddenly reacted, not with an answer but with a greeting to his former child parishioner, sung in the loudest voice possible, which rang out above all the nocturnal sounds: "*Salve in domino, salve in domino, salve, salve!*"

As the evening wore on, the two of them talked more and more, and not until the end of the week, when he was flying home, did Gregor realize that that had been the only real conversation, person to person, he'd had during his entire time in the land of his birth (the news of his brother's death and immediate consignment to the earth that he shared with his sister in the hour before his departure in no way counted as a "conversation").

Yet, even after the dishes had long since been whisked away, it never occurred to either of the two men, sitting next to each other at their separate tables—to the former pastor perhaps even less than to the one-man-expedition leader—that they could continue their conversation at one table. How fast the old priest had eaten, as if in haste, paying no attention to what was on his plate! And the man at the next table, whose one eye widened precisely when he was having a meal—at least the kind whose tastiness made that possible and contributed to the effect—recalled, as he observed this rapid, down-the-hatch, let's-make-this-disappear performance, that long ago, when he'd still been in charge of the parish, the priest would take his usual seat at noon in the tavern, in the corner with the house altar, and just as he was doing with this supper, *simili modo*, not so much consume or savor the meal as dispatch it. How this priest had rushed to free himself of the burdensome duty of eating lunch so he could set out to attend to entirely different duties, even those well-nigh impossible to fulfill, as often happened, and as in the course of time became the rule rather than the exception, or could only appear to be fulfilled. But wasn't mere "appearance" "something," something after all?

Not a word about the upcoming baptism. Also no question from the priest about his "dear Gregor's" pitch-black sunglasses in the middle of the night. (By the way, when the latter was greeted from the next table, the white clerical collar had flashed at him out of the semidarkness, as if the other man, a guest like him, were still in office—and wasn't that in fact the case?)

The conversation from table to table began with Gregor's asking whether the retired priest missed his profession. "I don't miss any of it—not the sermons, especially not the references, always in demand, to the relevance of the 'joyful tidings' to current events—and not the professions of faith, especially faith in the eternal life ('a' rather than 'the' would be acceptable to me)—I don't miss any of that. Or, rather, I do miss some of it: praying in unison, out loud! Nowadays, whenever I have to pray alone, for myself, and necessarily in total silence, I find myself, who knows why, wishing, yes, wishing that while passing a stand at the market I might nab a piece of fruit, just one, a kiwi or a prune would do. Anything not to be forced to pray alone, especially not the

Lord's Prayer! Better to be a fruit thief with followers than a solitary pray-er, deserted by God and the world! And something else I miss: being the one in the Mass who leads the other celebrants in praying, 'Lift up your hearts! *Sursum corda!*,' to which the congregation responds, 'We lift them up to the Lord!' And then there's something else I miss, and that's what causes me the most pain: in the course of the Mass, being the one who propagates what truly matters, more than the Mass itself or any professions of faith: the transubstantiation, not merely of the 'bread' into the body of Christ, and not merely of the 'wine' into the blood of Christ, but beyond that the pure transubstantiation without which there can be no life of life. Without that, the transubstantiation, no 'eternal life.' See how much I miss in my retirement! Yes, and see what else I miss: the gatherings of the congregation after the Eucharist, the celebration of the Mass, in the garden behind the old church. And now look, listen, something else: at the end of the Mass, before the blessing of the congregation—'Go in peace!'—the reading aloud of the litany of the names of those who left us during the week, meaning those who died, because—please, don't laugh—of the sound of most of those names, so much longer than ours, and so beautifully foreign, coming from my mouth, even if I've mispronounced them, echoing through the nave, as if from an unknown continent."

After the two of them had raised their glasses to each other from table to table, the retired priest continued: "Word has reached me that your brother has finally accomplished what he planned almost from the beginning, when he was still hardly more than a child—namely, has found a woman with whom to spend his life, or the woman found him. You're the only one who still communicates with our Hans. Tell me: what do you know? Give me a full report!"

The one at the other table replied, "There's nothing to report. All I know is what my brother told me over the telephone, stammering, shouting, gushing."

"Don't say anything against gushing. Doesn't it take good forms as well as bad?"

"Before that, I'd never heard Hans gush about anything, in either form. His enthusiasm for our family, our clan, our 'lineage,' wasn't something he gushed over but was, rather, a daydream, yet a completely practical one. His gushing—and I insist on that word, which in this connection I experienced as lovely, and not merely the word itself—was something else again. It emerged out of the moment, and once that passed it was over, no gushing ever again; but his gushing had to do with something durable. What my brother was gushing about would last, no matter what. Nothing would ever cause him to doubt whether the woman was, and is, the one. His first infatuation, coming not that early in life, would also be his last."

"And what did he gush over?"

"Nothing, nothing at all. At least, not over any actions on her or his part. Over nothing but their lying together. Over their mutual tiredness when they first met. Over the way they had walked at the same pace in the crowd, not only equally slowly but in the same way in all respects, not making any noise, taking no large steps but also no small ones, without any change of pace, without pausing, without stopping, and on and on, both tired to the same degree, which was what first made them notice each other: Eek! Two people not wearing masks! A question for you: do retired priests ever go to the movies?"

"I've just come from there. Why do you ask?"

"Because I've just been reminded of an exchange in an old film, in which a rather tired man is trying to keep a rather drunk woman at arm's length, and she replies, 'A tired man and a drunk woman: what a good couple that will make!'"

"Rita Hayworth to Glenn Ford!"

"On top of that nonsense, more nonsense just came to me, as often happens when I get serious about something: 'A tired man and a tired woman: that will add up not just to a good couple but to a very promising one!'"

"Who says that?"

"I'm not saying."

"All the better. Enough of that, now. Let me drink to your brother's love!"

After that, nothing but the whooshing of a tree, and then a second one, and a third, and after that all around them, as if a kind of whirlwind was blowing around the square. Gregor almost felt the urge to spout more nonsense to break the silence, to tell the stupidest jokes he knew. Instead, he suddenly got up to go, and asked the old priest for his blessing. No astonishment on the priest's part that such a thing should be asked of him, or on the other man's part at the priest's prompt assent. Then, with both of them on their feet, facing each other, the blessing: "I bless you in the name of the Father, the Son, and the Holy Spirit. Go in peace!" And the recipient of the blessing made the sign of the cross, and each of them went on his way, whatever that might be. From their corner in the shadow of a tree, an echo of the words spoken by a dying man in an old book: "All is mercy," and then "Mercy is all."

A moonless night. But as soon as that occurred to him, he seemed to see the moon: full. Somewhere in the distance, a streetcar was passing, and he felt as if it were pulling him along. Remarkable the way the usual nocturnal sounds of train cars' rattling and locomotives' whistling seemed to have been taken over, at least for this one night, by the buzzing, humming, and clanging of the streetcars. And then, high in the sky, the hum of a late plane as a delayed echo of the streetcar, now vanished behind the high-rises. A sensation of a breeze in his armpits. A candle burning steadily in a window. A dog sniffing the backs of his knees and then recoiling, its coat bristling: "You again! And why so fearful?"

Midnight was still a good hour away, and he remembered from his days as a student how he'd put off returning to his inhospitable rented rooms, different ones every year, all of them far out on the edges of town. And since he lacked both the money and the inclination to seek refuge in the few cafés still open at that hour, the only way to avoid going back to his lodgings seemed to be riding aimlessly back and forth, switching from one line to another, on the next-to-last and last streetcars, with the last one on the line heading toward his miserable room the only one he couldn't afford to miss. At the time, none of the streetcars, especially those with routes limited to the center of town, meant anything to him, except when it came to those pre-midnight trips from one last stop to the other, out to the city limits, and perhaps a short stretch beyond; in the end, he was often alone in the car with the driver, feeling something like the breath of travel, not just at his back but all around him. Now, as he passed a stop where the very last car happened to be waiting, he got on and sat down, far from the driver, in the last row, and again he remained the only passenger, if only for two or three stops.

In the beginning he'd kept his eyes, his eye, open, not for looking out but rather for enjoying the sight of the rows of empty seats, row after row of emptiness. Enjoying? Yes, enjoying. Enjoying the emptiness? Yes, enjoying all the empty rows. But then—from which stop on?—the eyes of Gregor the watchful, the one good eye behind the dark glasses, must have closed, and then—when?—he must have fallen asleep.

When he woke up, awakened by the silence all around, he found himself in the darkened streetcar, slumped down on the back row of seats. The only light, very dim, came from outside the car, from night lighting on the walls of the trolley barn. Was it possible? How could it have happened? Possible or not: he'd been forgotten. It felt as if, forgotten, including by himself, he'd slept for a long time, a very long time, but according to the clock over the barn door it was just a bit after midnight, and his sleep, measured by the current official time, had lasted only three minutes. That was sufficient, however, for him, finally doing justice to his name, to be wide awake, fanned furthermore by the draft coming in the streetcar's door, which had been left open. It, too, forgotten? Perhaps on purpose? The effect of the blessing? (And again, a burst of laughter.)

Why not go to the door now and leave the barn, likewise wide open, no matter in what direction? But he stayed, feeling comfortable, almost coddled, yet at the same time, in some unclear way, challenged, there and then, on the middle seat of the last row. Something was going to happen. But nothing happened. Nothing, and again nothing. Sitting there bolt upright, in the posture he'd assumed upon being startled out of his ever-so-brief sleep, he remembered that a little while ago, in the other part of the world, he'd been rereading the *Odyssey*. And now, unbidden, the section he'd been reading scrolled before what had at one time been called "his inner eye," especially the scene in which Odysseus, disguised as a disheveled old beggar, is taken in for the night by his Penelope at their palace in Ithaka, and after a day filled with humiliations, gradually, for a long stretch of hexameters, prepares to go to bed, or alternatively is prepared for bed by a kindly maid.

This old woman, a sort of nursemaid, recognizes in the beggar her lord Odysseus, the belated homecomer, who wishes his identity to remain secret for the time being, and the recognition occurs when she begins to wash his feet before bed and sees the scar from a wound inflicted years earlier by a wild boar. In her sweet state of shock, she knocks over the basin of water and runs to get fresh water, sworn to silence by Odysseus. The sleeping place he's assigned as a ragged beggar is in an antechamber of the royal palace and contains only a chair—a "double-seated" one, without any padding—with a simple bull's hide as a blanket. But at least there's a fireplace in this antechamber, and in the maid's absence Odysseus pulls the chair closer to the fire to warm himself. After hurrying back, the maid resumes her slow, careful foot-washing—with warm water this time?—and then begins to anoint the feet of her master—home after how many years, even decades?—with real local oil—pressed from Ithakan olives? Did the good old maid, whose name was Eurycleia, by the way, the "one praised far and wide," run off again to drag a second double-seated chair from another antechamber so her lord could stretch out to sleep instead of curling up on the single chair, which was far too short, and not only for her Odysseus? No mention of such a thing in the original text? So what? And did Eurycleia—a name to be repeated softly, all night long, until golden-throned Eos, goddess of the dawn, appeared—as her master, the false beggar, stretched out, on the threshold of sleep at last—long wished for, fervently prayed for—first peel off his rags and lay them, carefully folded as only a good maid would, at the foot of the improvised bed? "Improvised bed, ah, dear, beautiful improvised bed." Also not in the original? So what? But the text does mention the mantle, the covering, which Eurycleia during that island night on the Ionian Sea folded, tied, and knotted with her bare hands out of the innumerable sheepskins lying around in that palace anteroom, the mantle she eventually spread over her newly returned lord, whereupon slumber finally wrapped him in its arms, gently relaxing his limbs and releasing him from dread. Dread? Yes, dread: that very word is in the text. Yes, and reflecting on all that, the watchful one in the very back of the parked streetcar—see the ancient Greek *"grēgoreō,"* "to watch"—was granted, after his first brief sleep (see above), a second, entirely different one. Thanks to you, Homer! All praise to you, improvised beds!

He woke up, not at the sight of the goddess on her golden throne, but at least with the first pre-morning pale-gray light striking his eye (as he drifted off to sleep, he'd removed his sunglasses)—and that pale-gray light was welcome, for didn't dawn, when seated on a sort of golden bench, foretell at the very least heavy rain? Or, worse, a gathering storm, with thunder and lightning toward evening, especially at this time of year, the last thunderstorm of summer, whose track was hardest to predict, breaking out suddenly, without visible lightning, and with the thunder still far off in the distance but a few seconds later already right overhead, accompanied by a cloudburst that made everyone sit up and take notice? Whatever the case, this gray, bearing no resemblance to a typical dawn and in fact radiating a light all its own, was a good sign, yes, and welcome, because "I have a few things I want to get done today."

What had awakened him, however, was not the rays of gray light but voices, human voices, those of women and men, echoing from outside the trolley barn. Still half asleep, with his head resting on his bent arm as he lay stretched out on the back row of seats, the only one in the car without fixed armrests, he heard one voice rising above the others as the old maidservant's, bringing the false beggar a fresh-baked barley roll (or some other kind of bread) for breakfast, along with a beaker of wine diluted with Ithakan well water. Curious how young the old woman's voice sounded. As he sat up, he saw that a veritable troop, if a small one, of people in uniform was about to take possession of the cars parked in the barn, including "his," and only upon looking more closely did he recognize, primarily from their caps, which suggested nothing military or official, and which hardly any members of the troop had on their heads, that these were the drivers, almost half of them women, arriving for work and about to climb into their cabs.

This wasn't the first time Gregor had spent the night in a public place, out of sight and sheltered. Once, long, long ago, he'd succeeded in prying open the accordion door of a trolleybus, parked on the edge of, let's say, S.—except that in the early hours of the next day he couldn't get the door to open from the inside, and couldn't "disembark" until the arrival of the driver and the conductor, the latter still a fixture in those days. That had been before his time as a university student, during his vagabond period (entirely unlike what his brother's would be, and in a different country), when his wallet—if he even had one—was empty. As he remembered it now, the next morning the driver and the conductor were actually flattered that someone like him, from a foreign country that both of them, and the majority of their fellow citizens, dreamed of visiting if they ever struck it rich—that a person like that had chosen their rusty trolleybus, parked haphazardly at day's end next to a cabbage field, as his shelter for the night.

This night, however, spent in a place off-limits to any private person, had nothing in common with that first one. Not only was this a different time, but the country where he'd engaged in this illegal behavior (or whatever) was also not foreign but his very own; besides, he expected, who knows why, and indeed always had, that people in his own country, whoever those "people" might be, would pounce more ferociously, especially on this particular morning, than he'd experienced in person or heard about from others: "We've got you now!" In which connection, he pictured or imagined or actually saw an empty bird's nest sail in through the open door of the trolley barn, driven by the morning wind.

Then came the surprise (for him "surprise" always meant a "good" one): that no one entering the barn pounced on him. Apparently, all of them, these male and female streetcar drivers, were used to arriving in the morning to find an overnight guest like him in the barn, and it was more than a game when one or another of them inquired whether he'd slept well (to which he replied gratefully in the affirmative). One of them offered him a paper cup of coffee, "piping" hot, and how could it not be? Then came compliments, again not meant as a joke, on how "fresh" he looked and on the "perfect creases" in his suit trousers. (Missing was only a woman's considerately pointing out an untied shoelace.) As they headed for their cabs, he heard a chorus of voices wishing him the equivalent of safe travels: "Keep up the good work!" Once out on the street, he remembered a dream in which the nocturnal bird known as the "solitary sandpiper" had been joined by a second piper. A dream? Or did I really hear the second bird piping? Even if from farther than far away?

But, several streets, riverside promenades, and paths along the canal later, beneath the gradually blueing sky, another nocturnal image caught up with him, different from the earlier one, something he hadn't registered before, in the trolley barn's dreamscape: among, or behind, all the tolerant, considerate, well-meaning faces there'd been one that, without grimacing, without moving a muscle, wished him ill, was a spoilsport, not only unforgiving but downright hostile—the face of a mortal enemy, signaling, "I know you. And I'm going to get you."

Years ago, when he, Gregor, was traveling from continent to continent on one of his one-man expeditions, he'd spent an evening with a bodyguard, and this man had told him about his special "bodyguard's eye," which enabled him to pinpoint in any crowd the one person who would suddenly jump out to kill the "protectee," and, remembering this, Gregor pictured himself as his own bodyguard and scanned the faces of the few and ever fewer people coming toward him—no longer any question of a crowd—sizing them up with what he imagined to be a bodyguard's eye. Except that it was no laughing matter now, even if he styled himself "the one-eyed bodyguard." For suddenly words came to him, shot into his mind, for what had been haunting him wordlessly, at intervals, after periods of carefree obliviousness to the world and himself, ever since he'd learned of his brother's death. "I'm nothing but one of those images that can tip either way, an ambiguous figure! On the razor's edge!" And: "Us ambiguous figures! Teetering on the razor's edge!" *Us?* Yes, us. *And who precisely is this "us"?* How should I know? That's how it came to me, as "us." And for a moment he saw a gun pointed at him, and already the trigger was being pressed. *"It?"* Yes, it. *And?* I stopped in my tracks for a moment, then continued on my way as if nothing had happened. I still can't believe I didn't collapse on the spot. I almost wished that had happened. *Wished?* No, not wished—demanded. *Of whom?* Of whom- or whatever. Preferably a stray bullet. And it—there's that "it" again—gave me a push to get moving, to speed up. *"Onward!"?* "Yes, "onward!" What a kick in the pants. A kick to remember!

He'd had a destination in mind, except that now, "thanks to the stray bullet," he felt a fresh surge of strength to reach it. And this destination was the last remaining forest, located in a hilly section of the agglomeration. Gregor had never gone there, less because that section, of all the newly planned settlements, was the farthest from his own than because for him, the world traveler, all areas in the immediate neighborhood had remained terra incognita. Back in village times, before the New Town era, the other villages in the vicinity had meant nothing to him, and that included their names: no rhythm, no resonance that held any promise. No wide world would open up to him there, unlike in the Aleutian Islands, along the Rio Grande, in Timbuktu, in Dar es Salaam. But now the time of neighboring villages had arrived, the time of nearby, no, all other sections, both those nearby and those farthest away. And it wasn't merely the time for different places—the Bering Sea for the Bering Sea tribes, the Texas prairie for the Texans, Terra del Fuego for the Fuegians—but also the time for a different kind of time, at least for him, the ambiguous figure, the figure on the razor's edge, and his story and that of those like him; for they existed, people like him, they had to exist: this is your moment, your moment for different places and a different time! *But what does that mean, "those like you"?* The ones who try to go their own way, like me.

Enough for now, for the time being, of the remaining days of his week in the interior, with the streetcars, bus lines, commuter trains, and above all long-distance trains, enough altogether of modes of transport and being transported. Just walking, walking, walking. *Without any breaks?* Breaks aplenty, all kinds of breaks, but not for resting, only stopping, briefly, perhaps also for longer, and then continuing on, briskly.

Accordingly, he visited not a few shops, as on the

previous day, or paused to look over street vendors' wares, also bought something in every part of town he walked through, at least one small item, more or less useful for what he had in mind, and occasionally a completely useless trifle, the one big purchase being a coat, part of the first shipment of fall clothing, being delivered as he happened to pass the shop. This was the first time in a long while that Gregor, who as a youth, especially at night, had often stood alone, staring into the brightly lit windows of stores in the nearby metropolis, felt, to his surprise, an unmistakable yearning for "something to wear," specifically "something big and beautiful," and then enjoyed trying on coat after coat before the mirror until he thought he'd found the "most beautiful one." Although it was a warm day, even hot, he wore it out of the store, draped over his shoulders, letting it whip around his ankles—that was how long this new garment was.

His one longer daytime stop came about when he spontaneously branched off, as he often would in the course of the week, this time to one of the stadiums, most of them for football, with which each section of the New Town was provided, somehow or other. There he chose a seat at the very top of the seemingly empty stands. It was late in the noon hour or early afternoon. The stands were small but roofed over, and, as he couldn't resist registering in his capacity as a chronicler, well matched to the neighborhood he'd been passing through. (Or was such a thought contrived?) When he looked up from consuming the snack he'd picked up at a lunch counter along the way and glanced around, he noticed that he wasn't the only person eating alone in the stands, though the playing field below was empty. Here and there, only now visible in the shadows cast by the roof, were figures, all solitary, who were using the stadium's midday stillness for their lunch break, and in one of the lone eaters he thought he recognized the stylish young man in whose store he'd just bought the coat. The woman with the Egyptian or Greek profile (Ithaka?), who, after she'd carefully packed up the leftovers from her meal, piece by piece, held an unlit cigarette between her ring and middle fingers as she buried herself in the massive folder on her knees, a legal case file: wasn't she just like, if not the very woman to whom he'd pointed out . . . when he was disembarking earlier at the bus station ("earlier"?) . . . ? And now the man asleep in the farthest corner, stretched out across three, if not four, seats, with a newspaper over him and a bottle at his feet . . . ? ("Now"?)

No: "Now" meant the figure that at this point, with the regulation-sized football pitch completely empty otherwise in early-afternoon peace and quiet, appeared on the halfway line in the stadium, as small as it was monumental, toying with the football alone in the center circle, on and on. At first the observer up in the stands thought he saw down there, practicing by himself, an almost familiar sight, a rather scrawny boy, not old or big enough yet to play on a team but training with that in mind; but then he realized that the figure—yes, that's what it was, as he could tell not only from the long ponytail swishing back and forth—was a girl, a growing girl, not much more than a child.

The way she was playing down there, all by herself: that was something the world, at least in his, in my, experience, hadn't seen before. *Like a man?* Nonsense (again). And if there seemed at first to be some resemblance to a boy playing by himself, that impression evaporated as Gregor continued to watch. No imaginary opposing player was ever outwitted. No kick in the direction of the goal box, and none toward the sideline fence, which would have "returned" the ball to her. The girl's play remained, as long as it lasted—and it lasted precisely, down to the tenth of a second, the regulation time for a game—purely and exclusively a game with herself, during which she showed no consciousness of being watched, even by him (who was involuntarily playing along). A game that for its entire duration took place in almost one spot, with at most one or two steps over the halfway line and back, the one exception coming toward the end, though not as the finale, when the player—whether with her head or her foot I couldn't say—sent the ball flying away from herself and high into the air above the stadium, and then, with a few steps, giant ones, as if to measure out the distance, didn't run after it but went to meet it on the edge of the center circle, and from there, a good second before it hit the grass, made it sail—*"sail"?*—yes, sail—*perhaps with an overhead kick?*—if so a very gentle one (Is that a contradiction? Perhaps not in the case of this player?)—I repeat: let it sail to the halfway line, where, in the next-to-last moment, she scooped up the ball on her toes, and, as if to let the game wind down, maneuvered it bit by bit, while her ponytail swished evenly back and forth, never abruptly, almost sedately, as it had all through the game. And now the end of the game: letting the ball be a ball, and beaming, quietly, as if secretly, to herself. A creature. Yes, a creature. And part of that was that she, as a solitary player, in contrast to the increasing numbers of solitary players on all continents, yes, unlike the others, unlike you and me, had nothing uncanny about her, nothing to inspire fear, to make people afraid for her and for others. But what was it? That, in contrast to us uncanny solitary players, she radiated something heartwarming, heartwarmingness as quiet confidence, which, thanks to her playing, no power on earth could take from her. It was the heartwarming quality that, at least from time to time, including nowadays, glowed in the corners of the eyes of small children who were not yet able to speak, only to babble. "A good game is played without words": one of the most important rules, and not just for football?

Strange or not: what additionally gave him not just a boost but, believe it or not, also momentum to continue on his way to the woods east of the New Town: that, unlike in the morning and the whole earlier part of the day, he no longer had his shadow in front of him. From now till sunset, his shadow would stay behind him, and he thought, almost humming the words to himself, "I'm rid of it, my shadow, I'm rid of it!" How he'd been hobbled, and somehow distracted, a new experience for him, by that shadow, especially the shadow of his cranium, its very outline "ugly," "lamebrained," nothing "classically Greek" about it. And the midday sun had done nothing to resolve his shadow problem, for then his accursed shadow, foreshortened in the late-summer rays, pointed in the wrong direction, north instead of east, and whenever the walker, under some compulsion, squinted sideways to check on it, it seemed, and not just seemed, to be competing with him for the path.

"Teetering on the brink," "on the razor's edge": what specific evidence pointed to that? What was that about? He had no answer, would at most have been able to mention one thing or another, nothing conclusive. It didn't involve some mortal danger, at least not an immediate one. "Teetering" didn't mean "falling off," just "teetering." He wasn't at risk of being prohibited from practicing his profession. No one was on the trail of all the murders he'd committed as a young man, if only in his dreams. He wasn't mentally ill, and it was no delusion that whispered that he was on the razor's edge, but also no devil, and if it was one, it was a devil that didn't really have it in for him. He wasn't out of control, hadn't taken leave of his senses, at least not all of them! As he strode along, with solid ground underfoot, he wasn't about to keel over. And who said anything "threatened" him? Couldn't one also imagine a form of teetering that would put one in a good position, the right one, from which one could finally move on, no matter the direction, just onward, after almost interminable teetering that made one dizzy? And wasn't there a way to sharpen the razor's edge to make it useful, for whatever purpose? It wouldn't have taken much for him to wish that things might stay that way, for him personally, letting him stay on the razor's edge, keep things ambiguous. Yes, something was threatening him, and, then again, not. Yes, there was danger, but the kind he could do something about, and it might give him a nice boost.

Gregor intended to spend the evening, the night, and the following day in the woods. Not that he expected nature to provide a solution or an escape. Simple curiosity? Something more was pulling him there: a thirst for knowledge, together with a longing for far-off places—rather odd, considering that the woods, though he'd never gone into them, at least not that he recalled, formed part of the landscape of his childhood, the part, to be sure, that most often served as the setting for long, complicated tales told in his grandparents' and parents' house, tales more the stuff of myth than derived from actual experience, and, another oddity, seldom announced in advance, as might be the case, for example, with storytelling after supper or on a special occasion, but instead occurring as impromptu outpourings that seemed to take the storyteller him- or herself by surprise, like certain blues ballads performed on the spur of the moment: Have you ever heard . . . ? Gregor had spent many nights out in the open, on one continent or another, but what now beckoned to him was his first intentional night under the open sky in his own neighborhood—yes, beckoned. Yearning for distant places and thirst for knowledge.

On the map, the woods didn't take up much space compared with the settled sections of the New Town, which stretched across the plain to all the visible horizons; the patch of green created a rather modest, almost inconspicuous, midsized island in the black-and-white sea of houses, along with highways, secondary roads, and streets. But that impression could be deceptive, and not only because of the far larger expanse of the woods not shown on the map, stretching into the hills, steep in some places, entirely devoid of settlements, rising and falling in a chain across the plain.

At sunset, when Gregor, coming from what he perceived as the west, had reached the foot of the first hill and climbed straight up through the woods to the treeless clearing on its crest, wherever he looked, in all directions, from the nearest to the most distant horizons, he had nothing but forest and more forest before him, as far as the eye could see, made up of every conceivable species of deciduous tree, and through the trunks and the crowns not a trace of a house, let alone of the vast agglomeration, and if there was any sound, only an unidentifiable rumble.

This forest, its trees standing side by side as if holding hands, arched toward him from hill after hill in the early-evening wind, and he was reminded of a painting from the 1930s, not its subject but its title, *The Entire City*, and in that spirit he now involuntarily named the image or sight before him "the Entire Forest."

"Never have I seen anything like this!" he said out loud, and: "Never has the world seen the like!" Was it an optical illusion that all the trees, including ones that were usually lithe and lissome—birches, rowans, maples—and even those that were more bushlike—hazelnuts and elderberries—appeared to him as giants, their bodies huge and their crowns even more so, and gave the impression that it wasn't that the wind was tossing them but that they were tossing so mightily on their own, and tossing and tossing: a hallucination? So what if it was? "This is a world-class forest, and the Bohemian Forest, the current one, the forests of the Hindu Kush, on the Yukon, in the Atlas Mountains, are nothing by comparison, not to mention the Amazonian rain forest!" And then, to his own amazement: how proud he felt, unexpectedly, of this world-class forest, a wonder of nature in his native region, of all places! And wasn't it the very first time he'd felt proud of something from hereabouts? True: he'd taken pleasure in quite a few things, especially with the passage of time and on his annual trips home—"But what did I have to be proud of?" Now he was proud, however, and it felt right to stand there, before himself and the Entire Forest, as a local patriot.

Not until the next morning did he plan to cross the forest, however it worked out (consulting the survey map only if it couldn't be helped). There was plenty of time to find a place to bed down for the night, so, going off on tangent after tangent, he circled the clearing on the crest of the first hill, which had served him as a sort of entry point, itself treeless but surrounded by trees, those, too, gigantic. No other clearing, not so much as a planted area, however small, could be glimpsed elsewhere in the entire wooded area. This clearing on the crest, however, was remarkably large, and it appeared, furthermore, to have been cleared not in the present or the recent past, not even in historic time, but to have existed, without a single tree and also almost without undergrowth, from the "night of time," prehistoric time, and so it would remain, with the exception of steppe grass and low-growing plants such as ground blackberries, into the most distant future, until Judgment Day, with nothing else taking root. It was refreshing, however, to stroll about there, with the vast open sky overhead and the light persisting in the circle of the clearing perhaps longer than anywhere else.

He had time, and hiked around the clearing more than once: the only time during that week of walking, walking, walking, that he felt he was truly "hiking." The hillcrest had no level spots and certainly no flat ones, was hilly in miniature, yet also unmistakably full of dips, dotted as it were with dips and hollows, most of the hollows funnel-shaped, ranging from small to large, the latter often having rain puddles at the bottom, and the largest hollow, far larger than the rest, filled to the rim with water, a proper pool or pond, its rim serving as the bank.

There was still time—"Time enough! Time enough!" he reminded himself—so he sat down by the pond's bank on the grass, which was less coarse than around the other funnel hollows. Dragonflies, often two overlapping each other in a pair, as if interlaced, zigzagged constantly over the water, still clear on the surface and to about a hand's depth, but below that pitch-black. They approached the water almost as if dive-bombing it, then brushed it—"Sustenance!"—and soared aloft in a curve, carrying a drop (or such). The single dragonflies seemed to have an easier time scooping up water than the pairs. Also, the countless water striders, mirrored in the pond's surface as they shot to and fro, their legs looking in the reflection as if they were running in the water.

He took off his clothes and slipped into the pond. After barely one step into the mud by the bank, he felt the bottom sloping steeply downward, and although he hadn't planned to, he had no choice but to swim. But the water was warm, even warmer than the balmy air, and he enjoyed following the trails of the water striders hither and yon. Besides, Gregor was the first and only member of his "clan," at least in human memory, to have learned to swim; there were several brooks near the family property, but none with sections deep enough and still enough for the local people to trust the water to hold them up; as a youth, he'd also been the only swimmer in the village, and perhaps even in the area, with its many villages and ponds.

From time to time, he tried to touch bottom—long in vain. Then, suddenly, one of his soles bumped into something, and this was a "suddenly" that instead of being alarming offered some safety. At almost the same time, his other foot encountered an object, almost identical, and, again "suddenly," he found himself standing on these two invisible things in the depths of the pond.

What could they be? As a result of his one-man expeditions, he felt fairly confident he was standing on wood, specifically a pair of round posts sticking up vertically from the bottom of the pond, or maybe that was his imagination again.

And this time Gregor's imagination served him well. For, as he left his standing position—a strange kind of standing, without a proper bottom underfoot—and continued swimming, he bumped, first with his elbows, then with his knees, into several more logs poking up almost to the surface, visible, actual logs, and in trying to avoid them he bumped into more and more. Some of them—just a few, toward the opposite bank—actually protruded out of the water, a rigid fin here and there, in actuality poles whose pointed tops, who knows why, showed no signs of decay, whereas most of the hundreds of other tops were moldy and rotten—pure luck that he'd found a footing on one of the latter that supported him.

Wasn't it about time to make preparations for the night? Repeating the words of one of his predecessors, he told himself, "Making preparations is inconsistent with the dignity of man." And besides, I have everything I need with me, and not just for this one night. But do I have any needs? Yes, I have needs, and how, perhaps as never before. But what? But whom? What from whom? Don't you need someone with you? Oh, no! Or maybe yes: someone to be with you in your thoughts. How I pretended to myself that I wasn't expecting any solution from making my way here, from this place in the woods, and from nature altogether. True: no solution. Expectation, however: yes, and again yes.

As a place for the night, Gregor chose one of the funnel hollows or hollow funnels; this one had a dry bottom and was padded with dry leaves from the previous fall. The hollow was the deepest of the dry ones, and in it he would be protected from the hilltop's night wind, gradually picking up as if coming from a different Far East.

Heartwarming words: "evening meal," "supper," even if he consumed who knows what instead of soup and what he consumed wasn't a true meal, or maybe it was after all? Then, when he left "his" hollow once more, because there was still enough light to make sketches of the clearing, its border of trees, and especially all the dips and hollows in the ground that mystified him, he suddenly recognized, by virtue of, no, in the process of, drawing, that what he had before him was a field, if not several fields layered on top of one another, a series, if not multiple series, cheek by jowl and also overlapping, of bomb craters.

These craters had to go back to what for now remained the last world war; the bombs of subsequent wars had bypassed this area, exploding at a more or less proper distance. Wasn't it more out of simple curiosity than a desire for knowledge that he switched on his pocket telephone's flashlight—its only function still working—as he made his way from crater to crater? At any rate, he told himself, it couldn't hurt if, before stretching out in the hole he'd chosen for his night's rest, he undertook this walkabout, unlike any he'd done himself and perhaps not done by anyone else, back and forth over the bomb-pocked ground, now covered with coarse grass, from crater to crater, each with a different depth, one rather shallow, the next one "two ladder rungs deep," the next one apparently shallow again, but with an unanticipated hollow within the hollow, and the following one with almost vertical walls, the rocky earth seeming to have caved in, forming a cylindrical crater ("Danger! Falling Rock!"), and on to the next.

And as Gregor continued to make his way back and forth, forth and back, instead of sleepiness—which he'd promised himself from the bomb-crater walk, though not really expecting it—what seized hold of him was the treasure-hunting passion that had dominated his childhood like nothing else. *So what did you find, poking around with a hazel branch, in one of the craters?* A tin coffee mug, almost the size of a saucepan, free of rust though very banged up, with the kind of tin handle you'd see in the hand of the hero in an old-time Western as he sat by an evening or morning fire. *And that was your whole treasure?* Not entirely; in the course of more, increasingly eager poking around, almost digging, the hazel branch unearthed in one of the craters a ball the size of a person's palm, and black—whether from rust or its natural color wasn't clear. Was it iron? I wondered. But if iron, it was heavier than any metal object I'd ever held, too heavy even for two hands—and it dropped out of my hands and rolled away, to my relief, because it could almost have taken me with it. *An object from an unknown galaxy?*

You're in the wrong film. At any rate, with the Western coffee mug in my coat pocket, I hustled away from my treasure hunt and ordered myself back to my sleeping hollow.

It couldn't have been due to the limited noise horizon down there that for a long time, as he stretched out on his back, almost the only sounds he heard came from close to his body, none of them remarkable—at first, only the crackling, soon no longer noticeable, of a pillow he'd made from a rolled-up newspaper, purchased during the day at another stand but not read, with the exception of a line in his horoscope: "Do not hesitate to claim what is owed to you!"

As the sun was setting, an eagle had circled over the clearing, mirrored in the natural pond, until it took off in great spirals and disappeared beyond the hills: Adieu! Then, in the last light, and later in the dark as well, to my regret only briefly, but close enough to touch, almost audible once or twice, something like the swooshing of bats flying by. Distinctly audible, however, once night fell, the sole more distant sounds: the calls and counter-calls or responses of what he pictured as he lay in his hollow as two owls, a male and female before mating, which then unmistakably occurred, with much squawking and screeching: Good luck!

Still not a sign of life from the New Town at the foot of the hill, neither the rattle of a train car nor the whistle of a locomotive, however far off, or, at least now and then, a car honking. Yet he knew that there were often long lines of cars on the road at all hours of the night, and many last and especially next-to-last trains. Strange how he gradually came to feel almost a craving to hear at least the siren of an ambulance or a police car. But nothing of the sort. And in the sky above his bomb-crater bed, no reflection, not the slightest, of the excessive light from the agglomeration, seemingly designed to radiate till dawn through the earth's atmosphere into outer space. And if the night sky above the urban area usually featured the blinking of moving airplanes and satellites, now he could see only stars, one or two of them also blinking, but motionless, as if on this night the starry heavens presented only fixed stars. Something must have happened—and extending beyond the New Town to the whole world. But what? He drew air into his lungs as deeply as he could and sniffed. Smoke from a fire? Gas? Again: nothing of the sort.

On the contrary, the air was cleaner than he'd experienced at any other time or in any other place, and that wasn't true only of the air in this particular forest. This air could be tasted, it embodied taste, with a unique deliciousness coming simply from the element itself, the element of air, which offered itself to him for tasting. Deliciousness, yes, but that could result only from a catastrophe, which he now pictured as a global catastrophe, something he would have welcomed at certain moments in the last few days. The war to end wars, the ill-starred war. The pandemic to end pandemics?

"But enough of that now. Back to you, my element!"

What followed lasted only a moment, but he was sure that, in contrast to what had gone before, its promise would remain valid past that moment, regardless of whether that promise would be fulfilled or not, or only in a month of Sundays. It was the certainty, while he lay there stretched out in his bomb crater—"the best sleeping place I've ever had"—"basking in the deliciousness of the element of air," and covered with the newly purchased coat (the brand to remain a secret)—that people were on their way from all corners of the globe to the clearing on the hilltop and to him, Gregor, keeping watch there and at the same time half asleep. *What people?* Those, at any rate, who meant no harm, and they wouldn't be surprised in the least to hear his words of welcome, even at a distance, coming from the depths of the forest, from the crater and crater-amplified.

No one came: that was all right and as it should be. As his eyes closed, one as well as the other, he thought he saw, in the eastern sky beyond the forest, Orion the Huntsman rising, the largest of the constellations, with the two shoulder and two knee stars, and between them the three stars of his belt, almost touching (as seen from the earth). But that was already part of Gregor's dream: Orion, the quintessential winter constellation, wouldn't appear in the sky for another two months. And as he was falling asleep, Gregor wished it were winter already, and worldwide—though, as far as he was concerned, the Southern Hemisphere could have the Southern Cross in place of Orion. And again, it was more than mere wishing; it was longing, and, as almost always when it coincided with his falling asleep, a special, even divinely, yes, divinely sweet longing, though the next dream promptly whisked him to a patch of forest with a soldier lying at the foot of every tree. *Dead?* No, asleep in a sleeping bag, all of them in sleeping bags, not after a battle but after maneuvers, and, from one sleeping bag to the next, soldiers, exhausted from the day's exertions, lying on their stomachs, perfectly flat, their faces, too, pressed flat into the ground.

After that, a dreamless night such as he'd never had; it wasn't only that he didn't remember dreaming; he also sensed, he knew, that he hadn't dreamed anything, anything at all, and why the devil not?! The dreams wouldn't have had to be auspicious, the kind that, according to Homer, can be recognized by the fact that they arrive through a modest portal of horn. Ordinary delusions would have been acceptable, those that, to cite Homer again, come dancing in through a portal of ivory—strange, but at least strange, right? And then a different wish—which had nothing in common with longing—arising in deep sleep from awareness of a lack: the wish that a mosquito might save him from this oppressive dreamlessness. (A prayer that went unanswered.)

And onward in the hither and thither, down and up, over and under, teetering forward and back, during his week at home: cheerful awakening in the world-war bomb crater. What had waked him, very gradually, was—you guessed it!—the birds of the forest, the earliest ones, followed by the early ones, if not those alone: with their piping and peeping, short and sweet, another sound reached his ears from high in the sky, the hum of morning planes, softened by distance, but soon unceasing, and from below, on the plain, the dull roar of traffic on the urban highways, moving rapidly but still smoothly at that predawn hour. A pleasure, yes, to hear while he was still half asleep this dull roar, echoing through the woods from below into the chain of hills, and, contributing to that pleasure, the occasional whine and squeal of an engine as one vehicle passed another or even an entire column. So no catastrophe had occurred. Nothing had happened. The planet still existed, and with it the world. The world had just taken a brief intermission for half the night.

Open that eye! What he saw first, on the rim of the crater above his head, lit up by the horizontal rays of the rising sun, between two woody grass blades, was a spiderweb, empty, with the circle in the middle—no bigger than the nail of Gregor's little finger—that would usually have been inhabited by the spider, likewise empty. The web was rocking, hardly perceptibly, almost in place, in a light wind, more like a breath of morning air, but sufficient to cause the web to be swayed back and forth and to alternate between disappearing and gleaming anew in the sun, so delicately formed and at the same time reasonably sturdy, as only a spiderweb can be. For waking up, in honor of your name, Gregor, there was this spiderweb, or wasn't it, rather, the contrails of the transcontinental planes up there in the blue sky, crossing and tangling with one another? Now this here and that there. And now both together. And now on his feet. And now, after a glance up at the contrails, tying his shoelaces, not too tightly—one never knows. And now touching his fingers to his forehead before the spiderweb, giving thanks in a silent prayer. Thanks for what? What madness! Yes, what madness. I myself don't understand what just came over me, given the misfortune that's pursuing me. But that's how it is. So be it.

Thus began the day whose first half, or that's the idea at least, was to become the half-day of his fame, and, what's more, a rarity for someone like him, on his home turf—however that's to be understood—and whose second half . . . But let's not get ahead of ourselves, for worse—heaven forbid!—and for better.

Before parting from the bomb-crater clearing, he swam once more in the pond; it was unnamed on the map, but he now dubbed it "Nameless Pond" ("Pole Dwellers' Pond" struck him as inappropriate for that natural feature, and inconsistent with the style of his one-man expeditions). The morning was almost cold—though there was no breath cloud, alas—and it seemed too early for the dragonflies, especially the pairs. Instead, while swimming, he imagined that the water snake, swimming silently at some distance and eyeing him, was keeping him company, and in the last of the skies above "the" eagle was circling again—the swimmer decided it was the same one as in the evening. He also drank from the pond: "If it's good for the dragonflies, it'll do me good, too."

After he buttoned up the "hot off the rack" fall coat for the first time, and stepped out into the forest with a formal gesture suggestive of an initiation rite, it turned out that, the deeper he ventured, taking his chances in a trackless area, the livelier the forest became, yes, inhabited, and not so much by animals—though by them as well—as by human beings, "creatures," the objects of his longing as he had been falling asleep the night before.

At first he heard only voices, from all sides, and a different person, or he himself at a different time of day, might have felt surrounded. But he sensed, and thus knew, that there was nothing to fear. Not that he thought of himself as personally addressed. But he had no doubt: he fit the general description of those the voices meant.

The voices, hidden by the trees, increasingly dense and tall, were of a kind he'd never run into in the woods. They weren't forest voices but—yes, what? City voices? Possibly. Voices from a sidewalk café? Also possible. Voices from an acting school, where, from alcove to alcove, from rehearsal studio to rehearsal studio, someone was rehearsing a part, and a different part in each case? That was the most likely, perhaps with the difference that this rehearsing was taking place not indoors but out in the open, as, for instance, in the garden of a country inn, with every actor at a separate table, under a different tree, or, as here, deep in the hill forest. But what didn't fit that scenario: these voices were untrained, speaking not in cultivated tones, and certainly not in a foreign language. Each and every one spoke the language of the region's indigenous residents, of the agglomerations, with occasional traces of the dialect and dialects of the many villages that had formerly occupied the terrain, traces representing the last inherited features, now almost extinct. And the main characteristic he detected in these speakers before catching sight of them, more or less one at a time: the voices belonging to very young people might be loud, but they were completely free of malice, the voices of schoolchildren, yes, though at that moment they were out of school, or not in school at all, of any kind.

In reality—"in reality" again—it turned out that the group, in contrast to the impression of many voices behind the trees, was a rather small one that had set out the previous day from the New Town below to the wooded hills, planning to spend the couple of days and nights before the fall semester going from hill to hill, from campsite to campsite, as a "research caravan," the idea and the wording having originated at the group's welcome-back party after the summer break (the members "in reality" not quite as young as their voices suggested—see the one or two "late bloomers").

Their first day of plunging into the forest and spending the night there had filled the caravan members with even more enthusiasm for their "research." But that had been limited to finding and collecting things, and no one in the group had succeeded in matching even a single one of the forest objects or phenomena they'd discovered with its scientific name, no matter how much technical information they recited from the many scholarly books they'd lugged with them, and that failure applied to the caravan's leader as well—to him most of all. "This is so frustrating!" "I'm losing my mind!" "Help!"

"I'm going to throw myself off Mount Everest!" "Who can save us?" Some of these exclamations, echoing from here and there among the towering tree trunks, were groaned as if those uttering them were in dire straits.

Who knows why, but Gregor seemed to have turned up just in time for the caravan suffering from hopeless object-word confusion, and not only "seemed." He would save them, and me, and you. That's what he looks like, after all, a born savior and caravan leader. And that's also how his brief hour of fame began.

Accordingly, to summarize: though he didn't know the nomenclature and characteristics of every natural object the young people had collected or observed, he was familiar with so many that when he identified them and added a few comments he astonished his audience, each and every one. *Was it his knowledge?* Nonsense. What are you thinking of? These young people's astonishment had nothing to do with admiration, nor was it the amazement expressed by the audience of a television quiz show, cheering *unisono*, so to speak, for the one quiz participant who knew the correct answer to every question, and instantaneously. And strange, again, that the amazement of these young people was often sparked by incidental comments Gregor dropped, seemingly unconsciously, or by intentional distractions he introduced, or asides he murmured when he was trying to pinpoint the essence of the object under discussion—an example of the forest's flora and fauna or of "in-between" objects—or was trying at least to touch on its essential characteristics, information that regularly escaped him, and that he thought, from the outset and in the last analysis, he couldn't be expected to know.

At any rate, before he so much as opened his mouth, he had a sense, who knows how, of a diffuse trust flowing toward him from the young folk, and this trust had strengthened, if possible, as the hour progressed, into something like overconfidence, the result of their hanging on his lips as a group. In his entire life, Gregor had never received this kind of trust, not from those who'd "followed" his one-man expeditions for years, as they put it, and certainly not from his relatives and household members, of whatever stripe. *Also not from himself?* Actually, he had, but when it manifested itself, it was an entirely different kind of trust, an excessive kind.

He had no misgivings about the new, inexplicable trust shown during this hour by others to and for him. In picturing himself surrounded by each of his listeners, and surrounded in a positive sense—so that, too, was possible!—he was infected, as seldom happened to him, with the general overconfidence, and suddenly shifted, to his own surprise, from invoking the natural forest phenomena in a kind of litany, along with a much longer litany of their epiphenomena, to making things up—heard himself coming up with inventions, one after another, and at the same time, another surprise, doing so in a new voice, one he'd never heard himself use out loud.

The inventions were small ones, very small and also quick. For instance, he declared that, among the many-colored lichens the forest-research caravan had peeled off scattered boulders or glacial blocks, the rust-brown ones were in demand for natural compresses, but the blueish ones, the crown of all lichens, were wart removers especially prized by older people, and the frog-green lichens, "more precisely" their flower stalks, barely visible to the naked eye (something that delicate to be found only in the lichen world, nowhere in the plant world), could be used to brew a tea that in commercial use had the potential to become the king or queen of all green teas on earth! Or: "If I had my druthers, I'd suggest—by the way, one of the few suggestions I'd ever offer—laying a path here in the forest and filling it with tons and tons of the unused acorns lying around, perhaps mixed with beechnut shells: a healing path for people with all sorts of foot ailments, who would walk on it barefoot, letting their feet be massaged by the acorns and the sharp-edged beechnut shells!"

Why in the world did his special audience respond even more intensely, or at least differently, when he launched into inventing and imagining such stories? And really and truly believed his imaginings and inventions? The explanation—of course!—was that Gregor himself believed what he was telling them; believed in the possibility of making tea out of lichens, in the benefits of a sole-massaging path of acorns (less so of horse chestnuts). And thus he even believed his explanation, really and truly, when, as he was talking, he bent down to pick up one of the first edible chestnuts to fall after the transition into autumn and showed the students clustered around him in a circle the usual mark in the light-colored oval at the bottom of the dark-reddish-brown shell, a mark in the zigzag form of a star bursting out of darkness into the light—believed that in this mark something was repeated such as no other natural object had revealed, to this day, in such a small and delicate format: what is called the "Big Bang" (or whatever), or the birth flash of Planet Earth—really and truly believed it, and his audience really and truly believed him, too.

Then the members of the caravan invited him to join them for lunch. The "road manager," as he called himself, had brought along in a rucksack with a "three-day-supply capacity" everything they needed and some extras as well, for the meal was not intended to be a picnic, which it certainly wasn't, especially with the addition of the edible items from the forest that Gregor had identified, as well as the fresh chestnuts, etc., nearby.

They lit a fire for cooking, which almost didn't work out, because everyone, even the one young woman in the group, wanted to be the one to blow the kindling into flames. Gregor maintained that the hollow in which they built the fire was a bomb crater, and they believed him, and continued to do so when he informed them that the pair of birds circling each other above the highest oak crowns and whistling were "eagles" (they were considerably smaller, actually kites), and identified the barking of a dog on a nearby hill as the "rutting cry of a roebuck." Perhaps superfluous to mention, or maybe not, that the caravan's provisions included wine, and that Gregor, a moderate drinker up to now, drank more than anyone else, out of the relief, and also the pleasure, of being in company, and company like this, and especially relief at being distracted from himself, for which it was high time, and which he hoped would continue to be the case, given all the unknowns that threatened him in solitude, and more and more from one moment to the next. Speaking in tongues, at last no longer alone with himself but, rather, to and with others, also in their interest and for their gratification: distraction essential—an essential distraction.

Couldn't it have been predicted that after the meal the caravan members, as if with one voice, from the oldest to the youngest, would also invite him to come along as they continued on their way? Also that he would promptly decline the invitation, with the kind of hearty laugh one otherwise hears only from children? That, too. To anyone who'd observed Gregor in the preceding hour, it would have been as clear as day that for this person, "you there," nothing that came along would make a dent, whether inwardly or outwardly, at least for that day: "Nothing more can happen to that one, our Gregor, today, and, who knows, maybe ever again!"

In a rivulet with miniature waterfalls that trickled down the hillside he washed the dishes, to thank the group without words, and then let them go on their way. And obviously it didn't occur to any members of the little caravan to say thank you to Gregor in parting, even with a silent gesture or their eyes, for the entertainment he'd provided; indeed, there was simply no need for a thank-you.

Ah, "eyes." Strange, or again not really? No, enduringly strange, eternally strange. Likewise, no one in the group had noticed that Gregor was blind in one eye, or, in the current parlance, "visually impaired," "*non voyant*," etc. "Is it possible that in your company I regained sight in my impaired eye? Let me check the mirror!" (But he didn't have one on him.)

And, again in retrospect, alone beneath the seemingly sky-high trees, it came to him that the young woman, who, when she saw him don his dark glasses as a playful sign of farewell, playfully took them off, had eyes not for a one-eyed Gregor but only a two-eyed one. And after that how she'd unbuttoned a few of the top buttons of his coat, which he'd buttoned up to his throat, and then promptly rebuttoned them, but aligned them properly; had the coat been buttoned wrong since that morning?

In the hour that followed, he did nothing but sit by the feebly smoking fire, leaning against a stump, with a view of the sunlit hill forests farther to the east beneath a cloudless blue sky, such varied shades of green, and at the same time, from one type of tree to the next, completely different—not just nuances—such as no other color offers.

Suddenly—but not the "suddenly" that prodded him gently to let him return to the action, to the present day and time, to "being in time"—suddenly the forest, which had so recently been his domain, turned into his adversary, and nature, which earlier had always held out a reliable promise, suddenly not only showed herself to be indifferent to him but, worse, became, out of the blue, with a mild late-summer wind blowing, his enemy: the sheer, evil opposite of a motherly counterpart.

All that occurred to him now was: "Get me out of here!" But where to? Anywhere! Run! That morning, in his gentle trot toward the inviting voices in the distance, with none of the usual forest yellers among them, instead of giving the bushes and trees a wide berth, he'd run straight through them, plunging headfirst into the area where the twigs were most twiggy so as to "finally be able to comb his hair"—and how soothing, how refreshing and revitalizing it had always been to get that kind of combing. Likewise, as he passed tree trunks, he'd let his fingernails be filed by the bark, first those on his left hand, then those on his right, with the extra-rough bark of the oaks doing the best job.

But now, as he was fleeing the forest, the evil forest, fleeing from nature, the epitome of evil, when he set out to retrace his route, though now moving mechanically, the branches of the trees and bushes alike, with no distinctions among oaks, birches, elms, acacias, etc., merely "smacked him upside the head," as the old expression had it, and not lovingly. And the bark, instead of filing his nails, tore at them, as if the bark, regardless of the kind of tree, had been transformed into stone—granite, limestone, or flint—as sharp as a knife.

He stopped running, abandoned any thought of a gentle run, and stopped. How helpful he'd always found it in the past to stop, especially, and nowhere else as lastingly (a word not really subject to overuse), in, with, and thanks to nature. But what about now? Previously, whenever he'd resorted to stopping for a breath, and another, and if necessary a third, he'd felt himself growing light and lighter, increasingly buoyant, and as part of that (Hasn't that been described here already? So what if it has!) the sensation of having solid ground under his feet—at last. Here and now in the forest, however: he conscientiously took those breaths, even more than three, but then, instead of the reliable sensation of floating away, of being disembodied, an abrupt feeling that his body was heavier than heavy, in danger of being transformed (a horrendous transformation) into something inhuman, something forever dehumanized, related to nothing on earth, or, if related, then at most and solely to the metal ball he'd come upon in one of the bomb craters the night before, buried under the dead leaves from the previous year—the metal unidentifiable and belonging to no known world, let alone a world order, if it was even metal at all.

"Devil's forest!" Seemingly at the last moment, Gregor had saved himself by managing to take one step from that spot, and then another, and so on, slowly, slowly. At any rate, unlike stopping, it still did some good to move slowly, slow down, and keep to a snail's pace; this let him blow off steam, for instance. "Cruel Mother Nature! Did you pretend to care about me for half a day, half a life? Ah, all those gently rocking treetops greeting me, all those tinkling brooks, all those reeds bending toward me in the wind. And today, no, not just since today: you suddenly turn your back, the most hostile action possible toward friends—yes, action! Only an hour ago I was still moving in step with the rhythm of the trees, past tree trunks, along palisades, the palisades of a fort, a natural fort, inside of which I felt protected, protected in a different way from the people long ago in Fort Laramie or on the Yukon River, and what's more reinforced in—in whatever—and now: the hallucination of your natural fort up in smoke, and in its place: all the tree trunks so devilishly straight, unmoving, insurmountable: the bars of a natural dungeon, the dungeon called 'Mother Nature.' Mother N., I herewith declare myself free of you, from today on I am your child no longer!"

Had this declaration helped him get it off his chest? Not at all. Little by little he'd failed to maintain his slow and steady pace and was alternating between speeding up and faltering, but then sped up more and more, teetering on the verge of general panic, he, who in the midst of a panic-stricken world had always been the picture of calm. Bring it on, that panic-stricken world! But he remained surrounded by profound peace, to which the distant siren down below in the New Town contributed, signaling the end of the workday. "Cease peace" as the evil opposite of a "ceasefire."

A wild dove, an enormous one, burst out of a bush, and how he would have welcomed having the heavy bird crash into his skull then and there! Also, as he stumbled past a bow-and-arrow practice range, recognizable through the trees only from the sounds—not the voices or shouts of archers but, at intervals, the whirring of arrows and then the pop of their striking the target (or something else)—he imagined or almost wished that one of the arrows would go off-course somehow and pierce his forehead. (One of the arrows, with colorful feathers, actually came into view, "for the fraction of a second," as it sped past the oaks, not to be deterred from its trajectory.) At the same time, as the descent grew increasingly steep, Gregor took pains not to fall, not out of fear of breaking something but because he didn't want to damage his suit and coat, or so much as get them dirty.

Once more, when he had long since broken into a run, among other reasons because, to put it simply, he couldn't stand the sound of shuffling through fallen leaves that had once given him such pleasure, "my shuffling," "good old shuffling"—once more Gregor hesitated and involuntarily stopped in his tracks mid-slope. From the top to the bottom of the slope, pits had been hacked or shoveled out, at considerable but regular intervals, fairly deep rectangles, as if each were intended for an adult body. But the pits were too deep for sleeping in; they appeared to be empty graves, and not only at first sight, though it was impossible to tell whether bodies had already occupied them or whether these open graves dotting the slope had been shoveled in anticipation, so to speak, and were still waiting, so to speak, for their occupants.

In reality, of course, as it dawned on Gregor little by little, the pits had all been dug, shoveled with their own hands, by members of one of the local teams of forest-and-mountain bikers, to create ramps for dirt jumping, one jump after another down the slope. Nevertheless, he couldn't help looking down into pit after pit, seeing them as empty graves for soldiers. No matter that, as dusk began to fall, the entire dirt-jumping team sped by, missing him by a handsbreadth, one jumper per second; he didn't budge from the side of his pit, not by so much as a finger's length.

"No forest ever again! Where can they be found nowadays, the inexplicable, delightful, fairy-tale beauties, those thingamajigs, pure and unadulterated, from the forests of yore? Nothing but poisonous growths in the shade of these trees, the Devil's boletus—yes, if only they were *deadly* poisonous, but even they offer no certainty. And only Asian hornets now instead of our native ones. Where have you gone, natives? And only bagpipe players, maybe even in authentic Scottish kilts, in place of the lone piper at the break of day, instead of the jay cawing at noon, instead of the raven's triad at day's end—pardon me for comparing evil nature to you! No forest ever again, whether high forest or low, cedars of Lebanon or cedars of the Atlas! This is war on Mother Nature!"

In the meantime, to put the grave pits behind him, he'd broken into a run again, and overtaken all the joggers, of whom he saw more and more as he approached the bottom of the hill, running headfirst and headlong out of the forest, forbidding himself even a glance over his shoulder, down, out, and into the New Town, faster, faster! Soon it would be too late, and nothing would be open to him, Gregor, nothing in the world, nothing on earth!

What a sense of freedom—more than mere relief—once he left the last trees behind, and, finding himself in a wide, deep, open area, beheld, yes, beheld overhead, not branches and limbs, but trolley wires, yes, and also beheld a trolley, the head car sporting a power takeoff in the classic triangular form that glided along the wires.

Then he, too, was out in the open, on the street, a boulevard that hugged the edge of the forest, with heavy early-evening traffic and crowds of pedestrians on the nice, wide sidewalk. With proper ground underfoot at last, firm and hard, he was greeted by asphalt and returned the greeting. Good to see you, pavement! At the same time, as he was swept along with the crowd, from street to street, from side street to side street, and in between from pedestrian zone to pedestrian zone, he couldn't get out of his head a line that went this way: "In dry leaves your shuffle and on pavement your stride."

On a whim, he turned off and popped into the first tavern, bar, eatery he came upon, and even before he'd pulled the door open—after trying to push it first—he knew where he'd be spending the next few evenings before his return to the other continent. And then something entirely unheard of: he prophesied to himself (picture that: a person who foretells his own future!): "This will give me, Gregor, what none of my one-man expeditions has given me, something impossible to plan, a true jumble, unsuspected, not to be suspected. Ah, what a proud sense of self that brings, especially to someone like me, to become my own prophet! A sense of self, that's something I won't say no to this time!

Gregor Werfer did spend the remaining evenings and nights before his return flight in public places, primarily in taverns, with the exception of the night when a bed was made up for him, in anticipation of the baptism, by his old friend the former pastor, in the village church, no longer in use but being opened for the baptism of his sister's little boy. As long as possible, he would avoid setting foot in a private dwelling anywhere in the immediate vicinity or farther away, and above all in his family's house, his own! After sunset and by nightfall at the latest, he was nowhere to be seen on the streets and squares—"Make yourself scarce!"— and he further forbade himself to buy anything in the many stores open overnight, the idea being to pretend to himself, as before, that nothing had happened and that life, his own, was continuing, "as if nothing were amiss."

Accordingly, he told himself that first evening, after he'd sat down in the rear of a dining room, alone, or alone in the back room of a bar on the edge of town, or in a pub somewhere: "Here I am again, buying into the idea that 'nothing's up,' ransoming myself from . . . Yes, from what? Well, ransoming myself."

But by the next night he felt good about this particular ransom, and more and more so with every passing hour: "In these hospitable places, of no matter what kind, including ramshackle ones and dives, which may be the only appropriate ones for me right now, I'm where I belong, and it's perfectly fine for me to continue buying into this, seeing as I have business to settle with myself; I, dear proprietor, am not your usual customer but your dear guest, your partner." And the jumble again: out of the depths of sorrow, almost woe, something like rejoicing flooded over him as his prophecy for himself—"in the middle of an unheard-of expedition"—showed signs of coming true. "That's it. That's it. That's how it is. How kind people are to me, again and again. A person like me can't have it better."

During the day, however, he was out and about everywhere (other than in taverns). It almost seemed as though he wanted to be seen all over the agglomeration, from street to street, from square to square, even in all the parks, newly established from district to district, though people who knew him from before had never associated him with parks, or even with the word "park." The only places he avoided were the cemeteries, the many new ones and the old ones, now almost impossible to find; he gave them a wide berth, which proved to those who knew him, or thought his face "looked familiar," that he actually knew the location of every cemetery.

After his return to the other continent, when he thought of the Gregor of these last days at home as a public figure, he saw himself crisscrossing the New Town into which the former villages had been absorbed, as if controlled remotely, though also, in contrast to those who usually fit that description, a remote controllee who found his situation amusing, was controlled in a way that didn't steer him off his chosen path but, rather, kept him on it; good remote control; a gift that had come at the right time. So, luckily, he hadn't been turned into a machine? Or had he? If so, one unlike the dreaded kind that lacked the power of speech. Whatever his body did was of no concern—it was a good machine, possibly a blessing, sheltering him in its rhythm and thus in safety—though for how long? No matter: of the events and encounters he experienced during the day, in broad daylight, in the winds from all over the world that blew through the New Town on the great plain, he would ultimately have had no stories to tell.

But others, of whom there were not a few, would have had a lot to tell about those days when he felt as if he were being controlled remotely, free of the self-consciousness that so often disturbed and impeded him, saved for once from all that, a heavenly sense of freedom. And that wasn't merely his day but also, in a certain, entirely different way, theirs, the others', day. And who were those others? Impossible to say for any of them, for a single one. All that could be determined was who or what they weren't. None of them were his acquaintances, and they certainly didn't mistake him, Gregor Werfer, for an acquaintance of theirs, and he and the others remained strangers, even if they sometimes exchanged a glance in passing, or a word, or, very seldom, a whole sentence.

Without exception, what these people described were reactions to something he'd unconsciously given them. No: more than mere reactions—responses; understanding that went beyond a mere "Understood!"—more like "You understand me!" But not that, either: not "You understand me!" but simply "You understand!"

Those individuals wouldn't have been able to say what he understood, this "rather odd stranger" among the masses of pedestrians who thronged the avenues, but they could certainly attest to it, if initially only in fragments, exclamations such as "Disarming!" or "Well, look at that!" or "So true!" But then, with some distance, temporal as well as spatial, they would come up with actual narrative sentences, in orderly narrative sequences, maybe as soon as that same evening, not necessarily at home by the hearth: The person I ran into today around noon, just before the bells of the New Cathedral pealed, was apparently not involved in work of any kind, and not just on this particular day. But he wasn't a flaneur, either, and it wasn't by chance that he crossed my path, I'm sure of that. Although he seemed to be very much in the present, though not in the same way as most of the people you see on the streets, and his suit was inconspicuously elegant, if maybe a bit tattered, he gave the impression of having been blown here from a different era, and although he wasn't young, there was something of a lightweight, a Brother Ne'er-Do-Well, about him. But most of all—forget the other impressions—he came across as an idiot, yes! And a kind of idiot the world has never seen. An idiot I needed, without knowing it, or at least in the moment for which our encounter lasted. *So a useful idiot?* Yes, a useful one, an essential one. An idiot who personifies empathy. An idiot who radiates nothing but fellow feeling, inwardly, at a distance, silently. An idiot who, no matter what happens, never scowls—his face never showing anything but a blink of sympathy. But what a blink! *That brand of idiocy as a political program? The idiot as a messenger of the gods?* As you wish. More like a helper. But let me finish! Just imagine: when I turned to look back at him, I saw and heard the man suddenly sob, just for a second, and then it was over, but he sounded inconsolable, like a small child, or an animal. Unimaginable!

The evenings after such days of dissociation—evenings that ran till they couldn't be protracted any longer, and, indulge me, lasted till long after midnight, in any pub or tavern, as long as the main room could be considered a restaurant ("dive," even the term, to be avoided)—Sir, Mister, Señor, Gospodin Gregor Werfer completely present again, and present as never before. Also engrossed, also for the first time in his story, in transforming himself into something different from a "story."

Never would he have thought it possible that he—who from a young age had been obsessed with the unknown, the foreign, especially with experiences he could have all by himself, on his own—could become someone who, back when this region was still semirural, would have been called, or derided as, a "pub fixture." On his few remaining evenings, he became just such a fixture, and was more than merely reconciled to that, and it was clear that he would persist in this role past this brief interlude: without a doubt, after returning to the other land, he would be, and continue to be, in his own way a pub fixture, only in the evening, to be sure, but whenever possible every evening. And another restriction: the pubs in question had to be the kind that had no regulars' table, had to be "regulars-free" (on the other continent, that kind of table was probably unknown in any case, or maybe not after all?—the local equivalent?). And a further commandment he imposed on himself: Thou shalt have no regular tavern, no cantina (the term used in the other country), no regular pub, and, for heaven's sake, no "regular watering hole."

But how do you feel about this: that on the evenings here, wherever you sought refuge, the local innkeepers welcomed you and, until the last minute of last call and usually beyond it as well—no, didn't "cater" to you, but for a while considerately left you in peace, and later invited you to participate in the goings-on for a while, if not, as on the last of those evenings, actually urged you to pitch in, to help out in the "taproom," "kitchen," "cellar," etc., etc.?

How I felt about it? True: I can't explain why they accepted me that way, from pub to pub. All I can offer, by way of a partial explanation, is negative observations: the attention I received from these innkeepers—which had nothing professional and certainly nothing calculating about it, and that was true of the proprietor as well as the staff, each in his or her own way—was directed at me less as a regular or as a solitary fixture. Only now, a while later, do I see myself as specifically sought after for such attention. At the time—*That one?*—Yes, that one, I took the attention for granted, yes. And may it remain that way—*Why are you laughing all of a sudden?*—No "why." I suddenly saw myself standing there in the kitchen, in the Indian-Pakistani restaurant, way in back, by the sink, washing dishes, wearing an apron that was ludicrously short, like the one James Stewart wears when he's serving as a kitchen helper in the restaurant where he meets his future wife in *The Man Who Shot Liberty Valance* . . . And after all the other guests had left, I was invited by the proprietor and manager to stay at my table to watch the staff's "small-ball" polo match and then watch the players—the proprietor, waiters, and cooks—romping through the otherwise empty dining room with their improvised mallets . . .

During the first hour of the evening, it felt sufficient to sit there as a guest among guests. A goodly number of guests occupied the tables and were standing at the bar as well, but from his point of view there could have, should have been more, many more. "Get you to the Old Farmer's Inn"—not its real name—"whoever you are! There are still seats at my table, several if we squeeze together. And pardon me for stammering—I've hardly opened my mouth all day."

Weren't there references in one of the Gospels, the good tidings, to poor Lazarus, stricken with leprosy and forced to sleep on a manure heap, to whom Jesus promised that one day he would sit and rest "in the bosom of Abraham"? With all due respect to Abraham, he, Gregor, sat and rested, like a second Lazarus, in this terrestrial inn—nothing could be more terrestrial.

One of its features, among many, was that, at least on

those few evenings, each of the guests who wasn't with friends kept his distance, and even if a few words were exchanged from table to table, not one ever thought of moving to the next table. But from the moment Gregor stepped inside and, without a searching look or, heaven forbid, a critical one, took in the people inside, staff as well as guests, none of them looked like strangers. On every one of the evenings in question, it seemed as though the very existence of the dining room created the effect that when those in charge wished him "Good evening, sir," they were actually promising him a good evening, and the same was true of those in residence, so to speak, as guests, even if, at table after table, on chair after chair, the occupants either glanced up at the new arrival only briefly and wordlessly or, preoccupied, engrossed in something, didn't even register his presence. And the appearance of being welcomed, approved of, by the assembled guests, even more effective than being wished a "good evening" by those in charge, such an appearance, such an impression—of this Gregor was certain the moment he set foot in the dining room—was based on something that was inexplicable at first but then almost immediately didn't need an explanation: the interplay between the guests—on those two or three evenings, all of them—and the seating area—indeed, all the guest areas. Later, when he tried to sketch at least a few of those guests, for the *Chronicle of My Entirely Different One-Man Expedition*, intentionally leaving the images incomplete and in no sense (!) "fully formed," "recognizable," etc., just outlines, silhouettes, sedentary postures, and of the faces neither frontal views nor half profiles, not even a lost profile, nothing but single lines, strokes, oddly curved ones, some curves almost like garlands, suggesting shoulders, the backs of heads—a term unexpectedly came to Gregor Werfer the sketch artist that helped him pinpoint what all the guests had in common: "well intentioned." Yes, those outlines, those silhouettes, those postures, even profiles—lost or not, for all he cared—he discovered after the fact that they had radiated good intentions, also goodwill, and that's what they continued to radiate now, from the lines, strokes, and curves. *So on only one of the one to three evenings of being hosted and served, as a guest among guests, did you actually experience that, also under the influence of your dead brother, yet you speak of it as if it were something lasting, durable, valid for all time.* Yes, and? *All that's missing is your waving a banner with the words "Well-intentioned people of the world, unite!"* That would be lovely!

But now back to Gregor, the guest. On his very first evening in one of the restaurants, as he sat silently hour after hour at his table, sipping his wine now and then after the meal, one of the fits of ambition for which he'd been known even as a child came over him. (His ambition as a child, for example: to invent riddles for which no solution existed. Another example: to create mathematical equations with so many unknowns that some of those who knew him found it worrisome. Third and last example: to think up, for the classmates who saw him as a kind of child prodigy, games in which any path one took turned out to be a zigzag course leading not to a goal but only to culs-de-sac and dead ends, with no winners but also no losers.)

Likewise, *simili modo*, he now became positively greedy to be the last guest. And, as the hours passed and the tables gradually emptied, he began to regard the few remaining holdouts as competitors. In what sort of competition? Why? Because he thought of himself as the last guest writ large—LAST GUEST—as someone with power. *What kind of power?* Power to bring good luck. The last guest brings luck. But watch out: The last guest brings you, the hosts, and everyone in general, luck only if I'm the last guest—me! If someone other than me is the last guest, that person will bring nothing but misfortune. Do you hear that, hosts? No more guests, this place deserted!

What for a while was an idée fixe, a superstitious belief that he promptly saw through, didn't take seriously, a little game, subsequently turned lucky, including for him: The Last Guest notion seemed to Gregor, again in a flash, to offer a prospect for the future, for him, who'd now been roaming around for almost a week. An old saying—he didn't recall whose—came back to him: "I was trembling with eagerness to discover the connection," and he revised it for himself: "I'm trembling with eagerness to be the last guest."

And that worked out for him on the very first evening. Initially, however, he was the forgotten guest, the one who, although, like all the others in the room, he'd given the waiter his order, waited and waited, but for whom no food appeared. But he was quite prepared to be the forgotten guest: the few times over the years and the decades when he'd gone to a restaurant by himself, the same thing had happened, as if it were meant to be. And so, after he'd waited for a suitable time—maybe he'd underestimated how long it would take to cook his meal—he repeated his order when an occasion presented itself.

Looking back, Gregor wondered whether the fact, or the role, of the "forgotten guest" hadn't contributed decisively, on this evening and also the next, to enabling him to remain at his table, not being pressured to leave but indeed cordially invited to stay. First of all, he'd been served much later than the rest of his fellow diners and drinkers (and he'd also, in his ambition to be the last guest, protracted finishing the meal and emptying his glass even longer than his usual slowness as an eater dictated), and then, it went almost without saying, those responsible owed him, as the "forgotten one," some kind of bonus—how nice to see them recognize that! And how fortunate it turned out to be that he'd begun this particular evening as the forgotten guest. And what's more, in retrospect he almost believed in fate—saw himself as one of those with a fate.

But how many last guests were still sitting there, how many last guests showed no sign, none at all, of getting ready to leave, until finally he became the last guest of all! Wasn't this essentially a time, if not the era, of the LAST GUESTS, and the outsiders, marginal figures, warped personalities, odd ducks, and weirdos, initially rather few, an inconsequential minority, were in the process, as last guests, especially at night, of not merely increasing their numbers but also, *urbi et orbi*, turning up everywhere, and many—indeed, almost all—of them, if one looked more closely and listened attentively, were coming into focus as serious individuals (a term used derisively, and not only in the newspapers' local pages), deserving of being taken seriously as hardly any of the more "trending" types were.

But back now to the special one among all the last guests, and to his midnight hour in the eatery, where the lights had been dimmed as a favor to him, with soft light and the sounds of washing up coming from the kitchen, accentuating the stillness. (The episode with Gregor and the dishwasher's apron belongs to the next evening, or some other one.) The restaurant's curtainless windows looked out on a dimly lit square, neither large nor small, which served as the plaza in front of a local railway station—also dark, because it was closed at this hour—and the site of the weekly market. He heard the clanging of canopy poles, not visible from where Gregor was sitting, but otherwise not a sound from outside.

But what did "out there" suggest to the last guest? And how about "inside"? For him there was no more outside or inside. Or maybe thus: outside was inside and inside was outside. And as he sat there, he was traveling at the same time, or rather being transported. It was a gentler motion than he'd ever experienced (another first? yet another? another still?), and he wished it would go on for a long time, moving him along. "I'm in motion": take that in a different sense, fundamentally different.

What happened next: during this ride, scenes from his crisscrossing of the area on the previous days were recapitulated, without any effort on his part, inside him as well as before his eyes—by no means all the scenes, only a few, very few. But those few packed a punch. They appeared to him not as they had when he first experienced them, and they didn't merely appear to him in a different guise; they presented themselves as the real thing, the one that mattered, yes, the only thing worthy of being recorded and passed along, and they came with this stern admonition: The form in which you see this recapitulated, as a recapitulation, is how it was, how it is, how it will have been, you hear? And that's how it is to be, you hear? Understood, Last Guest?

Remarkable, or maybe not, that among the recapitulated scenes were a few that belonged somewhere else entirely, to other locations, to another time, or to one context or another that he hadn't consciously registered in the moment. "Do I live on what reveals itself only in retrospect?"

That's enough now, he told himself, of my first night of adventures as the Last Guest! And all at once he wished that the guests he'd seen earlier that evening as his competitors, the others, the other last guests, hadn't left. What if—after an adequate communal, unanimous silence from one table to the next—not unexpectedly—indeed, expected any minute by all of them—one of them, these members of the Society of Last Guests, had uttered a word—and what a word!—a word that had broken the ice, after which, obviously, from one table to the next, word would have followed word, making the story's continuation possible, then and thenceforth.

The clicking of the market-tent poles fell silent, followed by the rolling out of the polyethylene canopies (a reassuring rumbling) to protect the market carts that wouldn't arrive until very early the next morning. Time for the last guest to go. Instead, he matter-of-factly strolled into the kitchen, and was received in that spirit by the chef (or sous-chef?), who was busy making out the shopping list for market day. Or was it the night watchman? After the two of them, the guest and the host, had drained one or two more glasses, Gregor was offered a bed for the night in one of the back rooms—of which there were several—and promptly accepted; the chef, who was also one of the owners, lived far outside the city limits, and once a week, because of market day, slept at the restaurant, formerly an inn. When the chef asked which back room he'd prefer, Gregor responded, "The one farthest in the back!"

The next morning, Gregor Werfer, long since out and about again, wending his way from one quarter to the next, from one village remnant to the next (each offering fresh discoveries), asked himself how he'd slept in his back room in the former village inn. And his answer? "As peacefully as in the bomb crater. No, peacefully in a different way."

In the old bed, the only piece of furniture in the room left from the inn, he lay awake for some time, while a sentence spoken by another innkeeper, back at his post after a longish absence, a sentence he'd heard, or read in a book, kept running through his head: "At last I can be an innkeeper again!" Yes, being an innkeeper, a professional host: the perfect way to be of service! And what vigilance was required of a good host, the good host. At every step through the dining room, the building, the property, it was vital to be on the lookout for those who needed something of me, 360-degree vigilance, looking around and around, making the rounds almost exclusively with one's eyes, hardly moving one's head or body, with eyes in one's back, no joke (a lame excuse: "Do you expect me to have eyes in the back of my head?")! Imagining the immortality of the good host, of good hosts altogether. When I turn up next year, in the next decade, or those who come decades after me: they'll receive me, him, them, the guests after me, just as they did today—last night, one and all. Who will sing "The Ballad of the Good Host" someday, with its line, "At last I can be an innkeeper again!"? Thank goodness, that doesn't lend itself to becoming an earworm, unlike Beethoven's "Ode to Joy" or "I Am the Very Model of a Modern Major-General"; it's as unsuitable, for instance, as "Simon of Cyrene Helps Jesus Bear the Cross."

He was already half asleep when an idea came to him (see "Ideas in Half Sleep as Instigators of Action") that woke him up: converting his parents' house, long since deeded to him, into an inn, with his mother in the kitchen, and his sister (?) in charge of the dining room, already almost as big as a restaurant's, and his father? He wasn't sure whether he'd staff the dining room or the guest rooms, serve as maître d', or perhaps be a very special mysterious guest—most likely the latter? *Please explain: your royal line in a pure service role? Without any power?* That was the idea, part of which was that all those involved loved it. To continue: once he was asleep, in a sleep so sound it couldn't have been any sounder, sentences came to him, so clear they couldn't have been clearer: "Rope yourself to the mountain of the people! But where? Wherever you look, nothing but slick surfaces!" And, awakened for the second time during this night in the farthest back of the back rooms, which couldn't have been farther back, Gregor found himself thinking, for the first time during his roaming around and continuing to avoid returning to his family, of his future godchild, whose baptism was scheduled for the morning before his departure, and he pictured his sister's son growing up in an inn, helping, even as a young child, to bring out the food and beverages, clumsy and careful at the same time, and he sensed, actually visualized, his idea of the inn forming roots. *Aerial roots? So what if they are?* The children of inns can be trusted: they're authentic, couldn't be more authentic. Children of inns: they, too, live forever!

Before his last night, the one before the morning baptism and the evening flight back to the other land, Gregor's friend the priest, guardian of the space and the key to the vestry in the decommissioned church, asked him where he'd spent the previous five, six, or however many nights in his former hometown. And Gregor answered with a time-honored expression in that region, still in use: "*À droite et à gauche, à gauche et à droite*"—

actually, the evasive formula favored by the homeless, of whom the area had more and more. Of course, his friend didn't believe him—on the one hand, because Gregor's suit really couldn't be described as "shabby," having only a few minuscule snags and worn spots, barely perceptible to the naked eye, and, on the other, because the priest and moviegoer had heard that his friend had spent one of his nights in the Palace Hotel, which, long before the construction of the New Town, had been the sole building on an island in the river, very popular in its heyday as a movie set. That information was accurate, except that that one night in luxury, which included not only the bed, the linens, etc., had been not simply dreadful, compared with the other four or five nights, but truly evil, a miserable, wretched night such as he'd never experienced before, of which the only part he could have revealed—but to whom?—was the dream that he'd received a second message about his brother's death, to the effect that in the body of the dead man, shot through the head by a "stray bullet," the heart continued to beat and beat, not audible from the outside. And he, in his luxurious "sleep cocoon," à la the *Odyssey*, kept silent on and on, true to his hasty prayer, soon to be lifelong, "Come hither, come, Age of Keeping Silent!"

How small, veritably shrunken amid the New Town's high-rise buildings, the almost thousand-year-old church appeared, out of commission at present, or for good, when he, after another evening as the Last Guest, approached: it seemed to be only a chapel, a dark hut surrounded by office towers, some of which grazed the sky.

But how roomy it turned out to be once he'd unlocked the side door and switched on light after light (so the electricity still worked), and there was the Eternal Light, still flickering in a corner, considerably dimmer than the rest of the lights. How many people this little church could have held, hundreds of them! And look at that: the garland of flowers around the baptismal font. See how it concealed the cracks in the stone, the granite, which had split in a medieval earthquake. And over there: the many medieval builders' marks, not, as was more common, on the exterior walls, but here on the interior, the marks not just scratched into the blocks of granite but engraved, inscribed by the masons, each of whom had his own script and icons. And he wondered what mark would have been suitable for his brother, the journeyman builder. A plain engraving of a long rectangle: "This is my house!"?

Spending the night in the vestry, cleared out except for a few chairs. No trace of priestly vestments in the empty closets. But there, too, he pressed the light switch, and a naked bulb hanging from the ceiling came on: how it glowed! That, too, a luxury! And another luxury: behind the back wall, running water, a faucet, even a toilet. (As an altar boy, he'd never been allowed to venture this far back! In fact, he'd never encountered a restroom in a place of worship, and he was even tempted to spend more time in this space than strictly necessary.) And finally, there was the luxury of the vestry chairs, upholstered and thronelike, three of them lined up as if for three kings, which, because they had no arms, served him as a truly regal sleeping couch—though toward morning he dreamed he was lying on a bed of nails, with a blanket of stinging nettles covering him.

Now to the baptism: the family procession, led by the retired priest, followed by the grandparents, the baby's mother, the baby (carried), through the main portal, which was located on the church's west façade and opened with an entirely different key, after which both leaves were left ajar so the morning sun, as it shone through the stained-glass windows in the bow of the nave, gave those entering long shadows trailing behind them like trains, appropriate and "fitting for a ceremonial entry" (as the officiant commented later, during the festive restaurant meal that followed).

The family was used to Gregor's not spending much time in the house during his annual "home leave," but never had he stayed away for almost a week. True: he'd always kept mum about what he was up to. But what had driven him to roam around, driven him from the house, his own, had to be something more out of the ordinary than what they were used to from this son and brother. But even now: no questions. Nothing but beaming with joy on the part of almost every one of them, including his old father, who seemed to have shrunk even more, if possible, during the week. What a joy to see you again, at least today and on this occasion, before your departure, and looking so well. Ah, joy! But there was one person who didn't participate in the general joy, and especially not the pleasure of seeing him, the one chosen as the godfather. And that was the wee one, the child to be baptized, in snow-white swaddling clothes, from which only his face peeked out. But what a grim look in those large, staring eyes, fixed on the godfather, and on the baby's temples angry veins stood out. They were not merely a hereditary feature, without significance; no, these veins expressed anger at him, Gregor, anger in action, aimed at him, now, now, and now. And now the baby cried out, a brief cry somewhere between real and feigned anger, while his previously staring eyes lit up and twinkled. And now a laugh—directed not at his godfather but at himself, as if he'd just achieved something. But for that momentary moment what appeared as laughter had also been feigned. Barely a year in the world and already a player! That trait had to come from his unknown begetter, whose identity was scrupulously kept secret by the mother. And the godfather imagined pushing the swaddling cloth away from one ear of his godson, who had meanwhile been thrust into his arms for the beginning of the ceremony, and whispering to him one of the terms of abuse commonly used to refer to children conceived more or less unintentionally "in the bushes," a word that expressed almost affectionate disdain and partially rhymed with "rascal."

The baptism itself: like "something out of a film." If a scene from a film, a rather short one, but also preceded and followed by all sorts of dangers; a baptism in a war movie or in a story featuring emigrants, a hasty emergency baptism, also illegal, the godfather thought, with all those present still on the razor's edge and remaining in that situation, which included the garland of flowers wilting before their eyes and baring more and more of the gaping earthquake crack in the granite baptismal font. But then again, the deft officiating by the elderly priest. What a celebration. What a festivity. What a festive atmosphere, heightened by the baby's promptly starting to cry, as if on cue, not too loudly, not too softly, not for too long, not too briefly, all in moderation, after the baptismal water, scooped out of the ancient pond in a plastic bottle, was dribbled over his head and brow. And then, just before the party hotfooted it out of the baptismal niche as if fleeing, the moment when the godfather, as the newly baptized infant's name was being announced, raised his head and caught sight in the distance, on a crumbling wall of the former church, of patches of a fresco, with the fragment of a head leaning on the shoulder, it, too, a fragment, of his Lord Jesus Christ at the Last Supper: Gregor didn't see the head as bent or resting on the shoulder of the one to whom that apostle thought, or knew, he was the most beloved; to Gregor the apostle's head in that moment was teetering on the verge of tipping. And how the head in that blurry fresco was tipping and tipping, thanks also to its smudged, unglamorous condition. Hey there, ambiguous figure. Hey there, we're all ambiguous figures. Blurriness be praised. Good, beautiful blurriness.

He and his family, his small family, set out as planned for the baptismal meal to which he'd invited them, at a restaurant that had shown its worth to him as the last guest, as he had shown his worth to it in turn. The place was far away, but they went on foot, and each of them was in favor of a good walk. It was a long time since they, the parents, the brother, and the sister—(almost) the entire family and clan—had gone somewhere together, simply walking, straggling along; there was still time, plenty of time ("Plenty of time!" as a greeting). The only one who didn't have plenty of time was the old priest, who wanted to catch a movie matinee, but that was all right; he wasn't a member of the family, after all.

Gregor walked ahead of the group. He was leading the others, which his mother and sister noticed as very unusual, and he heard the two of them talking behind his back about how different his leading the way was from his habit, as a child and a youth, of trotting along behind. The newly baptized baby was asleep in the arms of his grandfather, accustomed from a lifetime of hard work to carrying and hauling, and the baby would continue to slumber quietly during the hours-long meal, the angry veins in his forehead also quiet. That, too, was as it should be: there was a time to be with a child and a time for a child to lie quietly in a corner while the grown-ups paid attention to one another. When Gregor looked behind him on the way to the restaurant, it happened, as it hadn't happened in a long time, seemingly since time immemorial, that he saw his father with the swaddled baby and his mother and sister with their once-fashionable pocketbooks walking under the heavens, and not merely his immediate family but almost all those who were out and about. *Almost all? All. "Under the heavens"? But how about the first autumn mist, or low-hanging clouds, and the rain that began to fall?* Under the heavens. *In dim light, classic for days of parting?* Under the heavens.

No question about it: never and nowhere would he long to be the last guest during the day. Now, in the restaurant for the baptismal feast, an additional element was that he would perhaps be the first to get up from the table and set out for the bus station, from which he'd come a week earlier, and from there to the distant airport.

But for now, time enough, plenty of time, nothing but the present, the gift of gifts. Without being aware of it, Gregor, seated at the small oval table in the booth farthest in the back ("in the back" again, "the booth" again), became absorbed in observing his parents, the future innkeepers, who, the longer he observed them, seemed less old than as he saw them in his thoughts when he was far from home. Yet he had no particular features before his eyes, before his one eye, nothing but the mother and the father, and each of them separately, instead of, again as in his mind's eye, at a distance, the two of them together, as "parents," as a "parental pair." But also, the father and the mother as individuals remained distant as he observed them, possibly even more distant than "the parents" when he thought of them far off in the other land. And suddenly he was jolted out of observing them when he admitted to himself, abruptly, and horrified at himself, as if admitting to an evil deed: "Those two, mother and father separately, as well as the two of them together, as parents, will become close to me again, as they were in my childhood, in early and earliest childhood—no, even closer, in the most deeply moving and terribly terrifying closeness, the closeness of dreams—but only when they, father and mother both, have left me, gone on ahead of me, into death." As if to make amends, Gregor leaped to his feet, about to hug his parents! When he did so, their son's sudden hugs took them by surprise; first of all, it was nowhere near the moment when they would have to say goodbye, and besides, no member of the family ever hugged another, except in a blue moon.

What happened next: the mother and sister began to sing in harmony, softly, softly, so as not to wake the baby, and so they could continue to be together without his bawling—a song, an old hit from the postwar years, with the chorus, "Never will the two of us ever part / We'll stand by each other always, heart to heart." It wasn't because of the song that Gregor suddenly reached for his coat, etc.—ready to leave. The song, and even more the singing, had touched him, coming at the right moment, and his father's nose had begun to drip, as it always did when goodbyes were in the offing, and his lips, shriveled to the flatness of lichen, trembled.

No lingering! After beckoning to his sister that she should come with him—which she understood immediately and complied with as if it was an order—on the way from the booth to the door he cast one more glance over his shoulder to his parents, and called out, "Till next year, in the old village pub—ours," to which his mother replied, "But then with your brother and his family!" and cast a second glance, quickly, into the basket where the newly baptized baby lay on his stomach—a good thing, because Gregor wouldn't be haunted by his face as an afterimage.

Not because of the rain but because of a long-standing silent agreement between them, the brother and sister walked to the next stop to take the streetcar to the cross-country bus station: after a few stops, the streetcar would continue on underground tracks like the Metro, traveling through a tunnel; Gregor felt a need, a veritable compulsion, to spend the last stretch before leaving his childhood home beneath the earth, and that need had communicated itself to his sister.

Sitting on a bench together in the streetcar station, three stories below the bus station, they were almost alone. Neither spoke. Should they take the elevator? No, better the stairs, there was still time. Up above, back in daylight, in the spacious waiting room, all the seats were taken, so they found a place to perch, both of them, on one of the wide windowsills. The sister edging closer to him, he edging away from her. Both of them edging away from each other. Neither saying a word. Something they'd never experienced previously: as brother and sister sitting on a windowsill, far from their own house.

Now he said it; now it came out, in the voice of a chronicler, like something neutral, something that had nothing to do with anyone personally: "Hans is dead," to which he added the few pieces of information he had, in the form of a report. Once that was over, he tried to pause, but it didn't come to that. It—another "it"—promptly turned into weeping, silent weeping—not sobbing, such as had come over him just once in all the previous days, over as soon as it began. It was a weeping that he knew would never cease, even if it stopped now—a weeping that no one in the crowded waiting room could see, with the exception of his sister, who just as invisibly and—a phenomenon for a woman whose every other emotion made itself heard in all corners of the village or the district—just as soundlessly wept along with her brother on the windowsill, and it felt as if an invisible third person were shielding the two of them from the eyes and ears of curious onlookers.

The first words the sister spoke in response to the news of her brother's death were "I knew it," something people often say precisely when they've had no clue. And then Sophie found herself remembering one of the many family stories passed from generation to generation, a story whose main character she now pictured as her younger brother. In the story, a son of the family, three years old and still deriving his primary nourishment from his mother's milk, comes into the barn, where his mother is currying one of the four cows, and without a word promptly scrambles up onto the milking stool, from which he can reach his mother's breast. "But no: that can't have been Hans, because when he was a little boy the barn was already gone—that three-year-old was probably our father; we've heard all those tales about his sleepwalking, and this story seems to go with them."

In the end, the sister commented approvingly on the

coat Gregor had bought for the fall, "which is around the corner." She didn't fail to mention that, as always happened with her brother and his new clothes, it had taken only a couple of days for threads to be hanging everywhere, not just from the sleeves and the hem, in this case so many and such long ones as never before. But that, too, looked good on him. And she pocketed the scissors with which she'd already started to snip off at least a few of the threads. And in the very end: "Of course, in your hemisphere, it's not fall that's around the corner but spring. But that's all right, too! Those spring winds of yours are chilly." And at the very, very end: "I should've guessed. Because, every other time you've come home, you've asked who's died. And this time you didn't do that."

He had a quiet night flight across the continent and the other continents. He sat by the window without once looking out during the eleven hours and thirty-three minutes of the scheduled time in the air, but also, in contrast to 91 percent of the passengers, didn't lower the shade after the evening meal; he lowered it only after the sun came up, the sole person on the plane to do so, while all the others were raising their shades.

During the flight, a gray-haired steward sat down next to him, like an old acquaintance. It was his last flight, and now, at the end of his life story as a "flight attendant," his final utterance was "Never fly again!" This sounded as though it was addressed not just to himself but to all of humanity, as a political slogan—a new space program that would save the world.

Shortly before landing, Gregor Werfer had another experience like those of the preceding week that he'd never had before: he discovered he was looking forward less to his house on the bay, once so dear to him, than to his neighbors—if not to all of them certainly to this one or that. And when, after landing, he took a taxi and then covered the last Arabic or Greek mile on foot, he also looked forward to the house. He'd left it unlocked on purpose; apparently that had worked as hoped—the invitingly open door had spared his "refuge," his "workplace," which after previous trips had been spoiled for him by a series of break-ins but this time welcomed him so peacefully it could not have been more peaceful. And now he also knew almost immediately how, where, and where else, and where, too, in this country, in his pine-clad residential community, his *piñeda*, he would try to implement his project, his business, his Auberge of the Last Guest. And the urge abruptly came over him to call his dead brother back to life. But how? No how.

THE BALLAD OF THE LAST GUEST

The time I heard myself snoring as I slept in the bomb crater. Attacked out of the clear blue sky by a butterfly. The day with no birds in the sky. The wish, as I put on my shoes in the morning, that a scorpion would sting me. The time I saw myself sitting, as the lone passenger, on all the buses with OUT OF SERVICE in their destination signs. Dreamers in the Middle Ages: how different they were from modern-day activists. Lovers of the beautiful: we're all exiles.

The time dragonflies raised clouds of dust as they flew up from the dry sand banks of the primeval pond. Sometimes, when Odysseus is all alone, he begins to tell stories, and who is he telling them to? To his own heart. The child on a bicycle riding uphill for the first time, standing up on the pedals. The missing and the disappeared taking shape deep in the thicket when a ray of the sun penetrated it for a few seconds, and they could be seen moving in the wind as light and shadows. To the other last guests as they disappeared into the night: "Don't go, stay awhile!": And what did I do to keep them?

Don't ignore the first drops of rain. The confused old men, plowing barefoot through the puddles. The moment when all those around me appeared as my progeny, and I as their descendant. "*Prochoé*": the word in the *Odyssey* that expresses "the surge of water crashing onto the shore." Passengers in the streetcar: with hanging heads, as if in the stocks. The passerby with a shoehorn still sticking out of the back of his shoe.

"I had no idea dying is so hard," said the dying old man. The time when I returned to the other land and for days continued to hear the sounds of my native language on the streets. I tied the shoelaces of the little child wearing shoes for the first time. Using apples to prop up the book I was reading. The water striders in the primeval pond as the forerunners of humans. People who've vanished into their own houses: not a sound, not a voice, not a single face in a window.

The tablecloths and napkins, still damp, kept by the host for me, the last guest. The shuttlecock in high grass in the middle of the steppe. For a long time, I'd had the idea of sacrificing myself for someone, but now it was too late. Seeing my dead brother's facial features, head shape, and gait time and again in passersby. Parents carrying their children as if they'd just rescued them from water or flames. All praise to the country that has unmistakable last guests, aware of themselves as of their power.

The last rain of summer, the last couple of drops

glistening on the asphalt and already dried up. The time I couldn't decipher my own handwriting anymore. The mayflies dancing by day in the grass, and toward midnight continuing to dance indoors. The former ski slope greening in the middle of the New Town, the stretch of country road on which I used to walk to school barefoot now also in the middle of the New Town. My true face: laid bare.

Roaming aimlessly, yes, but by my own choice. The place where I wanted to hurl myself into stinging nettles, but there were none. Never shake my head again at others, only at myself. No heaven left but the heaven of language, with a word in the right place as precious as an object in its right place? (No questions allowed in a ballad?) Nefertiti, "The beauty has arrived"—will she ever come again? (No questions allowed?) Horoscope: "What great form today!" / "Oligo deficiency."

Contrails in the form of snakes, and snakelike ribbons of tar on asphalt. From the dark interior of the streetcar, faces illuminated by the sun, especially Black faces. In my native region, "simple" used to mean "shallow," "cheap," "easy to obtain." There were still some people who cracked their knuckles. How good to be out of the line of fire! After the nightmare in which I couldn't utter a word, the sensation of my tongue's being stuck to the roof of my mouth.

The time I threw up by all the seductive entrances to the forest. Instead of sticking feathers into my hat band as I used to, now I chose lichen. A delicately inviting neon garland over the entrance to a restaurant.

Well-meaning faces: they existed. That I never notice pregnant women's bellies till I take a second look. "Hey there, next row! You're up!" A bird sound: "Yes, that's one way to say it." Children talking at a distance, not just when they shouted, could be heard word for word, unlike adults talking.

Loudspeaker announcement on a long-distance train for those getting off: "Check your surroundings again to make sure you have all your belongings!" No real work done all week, but exhausted every evening. Godfather and godson: accomplices for a moment. An elderberry umbel, a blackberry cane blooming in mid-autumn. The time when I embodied a motley crew all by myself. And somebody lost the sole of his shoe while walking but didn't notice. Lizards in the fall: nothing but the tips of their tails here and there.

A girl with freckles for the first time in years, and right after that a whole caravan of them. The trams down in Tram Valley forming a mobile village of bungalows. The cracked seats on the bus looking as if overgrown with lichen. Last guests: our future clientele. The remains of a dugout in the prehistoric pond. Sign posted in an auto-repair shop: THE MECHANICS OF EMOTION. One of the first long lines of wild geese wavering back and forth across the autumn sky: "So you're lost, too?"

Pleading, pleading! Where's our pleading gone? The time I heard myself stomping through the woods and covered my ears. The time I wished for a helicopter to airlift me out of the woods. YOU WILL GO AND RETURN NOT DIE IN THE WAR. Blessed is he who can reply to "Did you get home safely?" with "Why, of course!" Walking backward like the referee on a football pitch, and not only in a game. The time the sounds my brother babbled before his first words suddenly came back to me, sounds we made part of the family vocabulary.

People who get on the streetcar in the evening and sink into the last free seats: their sighs of relief. I set out with this thought in mind: another summer tale—but then . . . "Get out!" as a blessing. Dreaming, during my night in the church, that someone was sketching me. The proprietor who kicked a toothpick out of the restaurant while I was sitting there, the last guest. My brother long ago as a goalie, sucking on a lemon.

Ah, all the things that sheltered me during those seven days. No whirlwind in the woods, but instead whirlwind zones, lots of them, in the New Town, where the empty beverage cans rolled toward one another, clashed, rolled apart again, and so on and so forth, for afternoons on end. Among the cracks in the bus seats, the intimation of an eternal pattern. The long accounts in the *Odyssey*, especially of the evenings, as if what was at stake was postponing something again and again—for what purpose?—nothing specific, "plain and simple" one postponement after the other—storytelling à la Scheherazade.

At certain moments still wanting to run headlong into a knife—but none was there. Or "May a stray bullet strike me"—but none came. Or "To be crushed in a truck's blind spot"—but for that one week all the blind spots were eliminated. The increasing numbers of treasure hunters since last year, not only digging in the woods, but even seeking treasure between the streetcar tracks. Many of the newly built houses lacking mailboxes—but those of the abandoned houses overflowing. All the raptor feathers, always just single ones, that I gathered the previous year, including in the middle of town—and this time? Not one, even in the woods.

Every time during those seven days when I thought I'd seen enough, the seeing refused to stop. Not to be forgotten, in spite of everything: the burst of energy that emanated, and still does, from the leaves and branches that brushed or jostled me in the woods and elsewhere. Yes, come hither, Age of Keeping Secrets, you're needed—yet there were some things that didn't want to be kept secret. The time I tied a kerchief over my eyes and practiced walking that way.

What kind of tree has a crown that towers above all the other branches and is shaped like the wings of a windmill, and also spins that way, especially in a high wind? Right: the weeping willow. The stone lion at the foot of the baptismal font opened its mouth and roared silently, "Hurrah!" On the path familiar to me ever since childhood, one morning I took one step to the right and one step to the left, and exclaimed: "I've never been here before!" Let the thousand and one kinds of lichen bloom.

A bush packed with sparrows, chattering from morning to night, and not a single sparrow that let itself be seen during the day. "The last guest to leave gets something to take with him!" On the streetcar, a young Black woman was reading an old book, and what I at first took for her shaking her head turned out to be her rocking her head in time to a song. Daydream of a "shade tree for the whole family," ours: the tree all by itself, not yet full grown but casting enough of a shadow: "Not too large!" For "all of us." Another daydream: in the woods, and not only there, an "unlearning trail."

When, in the course of those seven days, I heard the rustling and crackling of a clochard, not just from what I was carrying around but also from myself as a whole. All the tables set for supper in private houses with curtainless windows: whatever you do, don't go in; get away from there, go somewhere else! And the time I passed some children, and the whole bunch of them, no joke, respectfully gave me a thumbs-up. And women still had runs in their stockings, or was that the latest fashion?

The girl jumping rope on a balcony—and the whirring and whistling of the rope, but only the rope could be heard, no jumping—when seen from below had the face of an old lady. The bar where at midnight a voice boomed from the television: "And now the final question!" In the lead-up to autumn, the leaves tossed by the night wind always falling singly, if at all, even when the wind was powerful, and in the middle of falling rising again: those leaves were saving energy, "like us, like the whole world."

Be the last guest in broad daylight? No, and again no! When I heaped abuse on the child, my godchild, lying there in his crib, it seems to me now that he chortled with glee at every insult. And the time my mother and sister, to celebrate my homecoming, began to croon "Melancholy in September," and I stopped them. The one patch of stinging nettles as tall as trees: "That's what I call a forest!" The passerby who said, "I'd like to point out where you can find particularly fine water."

And the way the old priest found his way back to officiating during the baptism—how wonderfully priestly he became, and at the very end his "Amen" with the longest-drawn-out "A." The woman in the newsstand to me: "It's obvious you haven't bought a paper in a long time." I stood before the spot where the mirror used to hang in my parents' house much longer than I'd done the previous year. The sparrows in the bush on the side of the road: an invisible parliament. My dream during the night in the vestry of the deconsecrated church: a blanket of stinging nettles. And the moment of the first autumn leaf pile, still small, and the child standing there, small like the leaf pile.

Yes, my godson would be a good thrower—if not the champion of the Werfer bloodline, in honor of his surname! To be a guest among others, from dusk on: that, too, part of "The Ballad of the Last Guest"? "Sheila says she loves me": quite different from "Be embracéd, O you millions"! To the other passengers in the bus station's waiting room, the two of us, my sister and I, mourning on the windowsill, were two of the beatified. Our orchard newly in bloom—but that was in a different land—and besides, that was another dream. Our dead brother's guild mark in the asphalt of the former country road, now the street of lost gloves, the street of wind-blown newspapers.

Yes, the echo of a good throw—even without an echo. The morning on which I intentionally walked around with my shoelaces trailing. The right woman would reveal herself—and the woman who stopped me was an ancient one who scolded me for letting myself go. The patch of lichen repeatedly stepped on, and how it bounced back every time, springing up. And how I looked out of the bus one last time and wanted to promise something to our windowsill, now unoccupied. Seek and you shall find: no, that wasn't it—how many places I've spoiled for myself by wanting to seek and find. The child skipping in the autumn thunderstorm.

All the beautiful women with acne. Lichen as edelweiss. My sister's exclamation on the windowsill, "Poor us!" The heartwarming voice of a blind man. On the map of the New Town, the name of the former rural area: THE VILLAGES. Ah, how, during the baptismal feast, I suddenly saw myself clamping my godson in my armpit and carrying him from the North Pole to the South Pole. The secret that all those on earth were created equal—O noble anarchy! When my brother with snow on his hat joined the rest of us in the rain, and how, along with the drawing of his house, he had a three-dimensional model of it in his other hand. A hedgehog as a Seeing Eye dog. In the rotting woodpile in front of an abandoned house, pieces of a broken jump ski. Just as there were "garden escapes," there are also "forest escapes"—raspberries, for instance. From the New

Town stadium, the voices of children, clearer in the distance than close up: "Bye!" "See you tomorrow!"

Brother, unsung—as yet. True: as a young man, I slept in cornfields many times, in the furrows—but sleeping in a trolley barn was new for me. Every year, when I came home from afar, I brought presents, and this time, too—except that I threw them away on the last stretch, dumped them, and for the first time in my life came home empty-handed. The abandoned church amid the high-rise buildings as small as a doghouse—but the tower, tiny though it was, a real rocket! And how hastily the football players, in the middle of the game, tied their loose shoelaces. And—day in, night out—the lichens forming "the other network."

Us "on the razor's edge"? And this cutting edge is inside us, in the heart of our heart? All those who've vanished from the "villages" since last year. The steamed-up windows of the last eatery still open at midnight—yet for a good while I'd already been the only guest: how could that be? And how I left my coat with my sister for the winter. And how the news of our brother's death, as we were sitting on the windowsill, caused her acne, which had disappeared long ago, to break out on both cheeks, and how I saw constellations in the outbreak, which made her even more beautiful. Oh, fullness of sorrow, fullness of fullness.

After fleeing the forest, fleeing nature, I could do nothing but rush down into the New Town, where I walked along the "avenues" and "boulevards" as I'd once walked along the shoulder of the country road, more present to me there than ever. How the old paths, now gone, were still there inside me, as stretches, as units of measure: the path to the roadside cross commemorating partisans murdered by the Nazis; the path to the bomb crater with the skeleton of the unknown soldier; the path to the cow pasture; the path to fetch milk . . . And if, during my home leave the previous year, at most every tenth passenger who got on the streetcar or the Metro looked around for a seat—this time, the year in question, it was every second passenger, no, almost every one. And the previous year, especially around midnight, the rats scurrying back and forth between the rails—but no trace of them this year—and how I wished I could see them this time.

During my week at home, it became clear to me that thinking of myself as a chronicler was a complete sham, a misrepresentation of myself. Ah, community of last guests, community of communities. Was the girl playing football by herself in the empty New Town stadium aware she was playing for the whole world? And is she still that humanitarian lone player? Hey, how my godson at the baptismal feast crawled to another small child at the next table and untied his shoelaces! And the way all little children sit, their posture and their expression looking as if they're in the starting blocks. Instead of throwing, simply winding up, forever and ever! On the windowsill, a sign—NO SITTING!—but the two of us tolerated without a word.

And something else during that week at home: looking in from a distance at a garden party, a woman among the dancers wrapped from head to toe in gold plastic sheeting. Yes, Brother, when you, the Foreign Legionnaire, were asked one time by me how you "made out" in that respect, you just gazed up silently at the sky, until I heard a sigh from you such as I'd never heard from a human being. And although we'd met in a third location, one that couldn't have been more peaceful, every time we were out on the street or elsewhere, after a couple of steps you ducked.

And how, when I returned this time to my home on the other continent, when the house came into view, I'd thought: "I'll never make it to the door"? And how I promptly felt myself striding toward it—a stride to be proud of. And how I wished nonetheless that out of the darkness someone would hurtle toward me, brandishing a knife, and how at the same time I was sure I would stop him in his tracks.

Yes, she who turned into my adversary, into evil Mother Nature, if not a mortal enemy—how in the course of events she showed signs of turning up again here and there. But what signs those were!: The one who'd just been evil through and through was working and whirling parallel to me, and I was parallel to her. The time when I, with my brother's image before me, felt strong enough for a moment to call him back to life. The priest's "Amen": "in a stentorian voice" (from Homer's Stentor). And the time I was swimming in the morning in the prehistoric pond and experienced the water striders as the forerunners of humankind, and the silvery snail trails on my hat and garment after the night in the bomb crater.

The time I yelled "You little spit-up devil" at the baby, and he promptly spat up, playing along. How, on the New Town's one short Metro stretch, the passengers underground, in direct contrast to the people up above on the street, all presented faces, of one kind or another, all of which told stories, like this or like that yet also one and the same story—accompanied again and again, in my memory, by the rats scurrying between the rails down there the year before: "Yes, those were the days."

A child, forgotten in the evening on his merry-go-round horse. In one of the no-man's-land-patches in the New Town, the gravestone, without a cemetery anywhere to be seen, the grave of a sailor, far from the sea, and scratched into the stone the sailor's silhouette, with his duffel bag. And the time I sat as the last guest at a wobbly table, and made it wobble even more, and all the fingerprints on the wineglass in front of me—the more different the better. And the schoolboy dawdling on the way home, shifting his school satchel from one shoulder to both as he walked.

September–November 2022

A NOTE ABOUT THE AUTHOR

Peter Handke was born in Griffen, Austria, in 1942. His many novels include *The Goalie's Anxiety at the Penalty Kick*, *A Sorrow Beyond Dreams*, *My Year in the No-Man's-Bay*, and *Crossing the Sierra de Gredos*. Handke's dramatic works include *Kaspar* and the screenplay for Wim Wenders's *Wings of Desire*. In 2019, he was awarded the Nobel Prize in Literature "for an influential work that with linguistic ingenuity has explored the periphery and the specificity of human experience."

A NOTE ABOUT THE TRANSLATOR

Krishna Winston is the Marcus L. Taft Professor of German Language and Literature, Emerita, at Wesleyan University. She has translated more than thirty books, including previous works by Peter Handke and works by Goethe, Werner Herzog, Günter Grass, and Christoph Hein.